CRUISE TO MURDER

BY ZOEY & CLAIRE KANE

ISBN: 978-1-938327-00-1
Printed in the USA

A special thank-you to Kat Lind, The Ds, Scott Paul and
the rest of Phoenix Prime. PhoenixPrimeRising.com

This book is dedicated to moms and daughters who like a little mystery and adventure in their lives.

ONE

The sun was out, reflecting brightly off two luxury liners that adorned the crystal coast like great white whales. Travelers scurried aboard their ramps until they were finally swallowed inside, where men in uniforms checked tickets. Smiles of anticipation crossed many of their faces for what adventures lie ahead. One cruise promised icy-blue cave spelunking and picture-perfect wolf sightings. The other, sea-bathing with orcas and dining on briny oysters.

Nobody would've expected murder and mayhem. Especially the Kanes, who had just solved a harrowing mystery at their new estate, Hillgate Manor.

"I know I've already said so, but I do hope you don't mind we're going on a different cruise," their friend Penny said, speaking to the mother and daughter who were anxious to sail away. The tall woman wore her typical shades, large and black atop a narrow nose. They suited her auburn bob and couture resort apparel.

Her blond big-bottomed friend by her side, B.B.,

added, "I have certain allergies to tropical flowers. I can't help it. If I even think of one I... Ah-ah-ACHOO!" she bellowed through a cupped hand.

Standing near their own ship's ramp, Zoey and Claire gave sympathetic expressions of understanding.

"The poor dear." Penny passed B.B. a tissue from out of her woven-straw tote with the shake of her head. "An Alaskan cruise will be so much better for her condition."

The Kanes nodded. At least their friends were embarking on the same day. It was fun taking the same flight and seeing them off. In the distance, Penny and B.B.'s cruise line waited just beyond the Kane's own ship. "That's fine," Zoey said smiling. "We're just happy that you looked into things with your travel agent and found the perfect destination for us."

"My pleasure." Penny pressed a skinny hand of punctuated tendons against her airy scarf. "Oh, and before I forget—here's a special brochure from my agent." Her eyebrows waggled above her shades, and she pulled it out of her tote. "It gets you in 'the know' on some of the harder-to-find excursions."

Zoey accepted the folded-up paper. She opened it up and read aloud, tracing each line-item with a glossy pink fingernail. "Shark Vs. Tourist Race, The Great Volcano Dip, Zombie Meet-and-Greet, Helicopter and Hang Glider Tango, Jonah and The Whale Reenactments, and—lastly—Extreme Sunbathing."

Claire gave a crooked smile, perusing the map of events beneath it. "Well, that's good for a laugh."

2

Cartoon drawings of tourists risking their lives in shorts and bikinis added to the fun of it.

Zoey agreed, chuckling. "I wonder what the Extreme Sunbathing entails."

A low horn bellowed in the distance. It was the Princess cruise. "That's our cue," Penny said, glancing over a shoulder.

"Have a fun trip," Zoey said, and each of them took turns hugging.

As Penny walked off with her friend, she waved her scarf in the air like a banner at the Kanes. "Bon Voyage!"

"Bon voyage!" they called back in unison.

"Be careful of zombies!" Penny shouted with a smile that looked sincerely gleeful like she believed it was actually possible.

"We will!" Zoey said. "If I see one with hair and teeth I'll bring him back as a blind date for you!"

"No, no. You can keep them all to yourself, my friend!" Penny then turned back around and hurried, focusing on her own destination.

"You don't think she believes in—" Claire started with the tilt of her head.

"Nah," the two concluded, shaking their heads at the thought

"Well, I guess we better get going, Mom," Claire said, peering over at the ramp. She reached down to grab her suitcases when a familiar voice interrupted.

"You can't leave without saying goodbye," he said. Claire spun around to see Lucas Stephens from her hometown's Channel 2 News. His dark blond hair was swept effortlessly over hazel eyes that glittered like the sea behind her.

"What are you doing here?" Claire said, her big brown eyes opening wider in surprise. The California coast was thousands of miles from Riverside, Indiana. And although Lucas had been a fun and handsome date as of late, she didn't think following her to say "goodbye" was necessary or appropriate.

Zoey looked at him with curiosity, thinking the same thing.

"I wanted to surprise you," he said before leaning down and kissing her red lips. It felt nice, like always.

"You've surprised me all right," Claire said, her tone flattening in disapproval.

"I-um have something to ask you." He touched his pocket that bulged. Claire couldn't help but think of an engagement ring. But it had only been three months! She glanced at her mother, whose eyebrows were raised in curiosity.

Another voice interrupted. It was none other than Bob McGowen from Riverside, Indiana's *The Daily Bugle*. "Zoey Kane!" Instead of his usual Canon camera in his hands, he held a cat carrier. He stepped into the group's circle in Bermuda shorts and a Hawaiian shirt, not typical attire for the business man with full black hair and a salt-and-pepper mustache.

"Bob, you're here too?" Zoey said with a little laugh. "Who else should we expect to see?"

"I'm visiting my aunt," Bob said. His black-and-white cat, Mr. Smith, peeked through the cage. "She's not doing so well, and lives close by. When Lucas told me he was catching a flight out here, I figured I should take the opportunity to catch it with him."

Zoey sighed. Then realizing that might appear rude, she quickly explained. "I'm sorry about your aunt. I just didn't know why you came out all this way." She smiled, now feeling more embarrassed. "I'm just saying, I'm a traveler, a poet, a wild horse rider." She'd also been married three times but wouldn't mention that tidbit. "You can understand, I'm not ready to be making any promises."

"Oh, I completely understand. No, I'm just here visiting family and thought it'd be fun to see you off."

"That's wonderful, Bob." She slipped a hand around his back and gave him a quick kiss, leaving some of her pink lipstick on his cheek.

"I know you've been looking forward to ogling some of the island men," Bob said. "I can't hold you back from an opportunity like that."

"Okay, now you're too supportive," Zoey joked. "Although you are absolutely correct."

Lucas cleared his throat, announcing he had something to say. All eyes turned to him. Claire's heart raced. What was he thinking? It was so soon! They weren't even technically boyfriend and girlfriend. And after being in a two-year relationship with Jack, a total narcissist, she needed a break as well.

"Claire," Lucas said, taking her hand. He didn't kneel. He simply gazed into her eyes with emotion. A light sea breeze ruffled his hair.

"Yes, Lucas?" Claire said with hesitance.

"It's been a lot of fun getting to know you over the last couple of months," he said, tucking a shiny brown tress behind her ear. "Have you had fun?"

"Y-yes, but…"

"Shh," he said with a teasing smile, pressing a finger to her lips. Surprisingly she didn't feel like biting it in anger. Lucas was always a sweetheart. She couldn't be rude to him at a moment like this. "Claire," he continued, "I just have something to ask you."

Claire turned and gave a pleading save-me face her mother. Zoey shrugged helplessly.

Lucas pulled a black velvet box from out of his khakis. Claire smiled to be nice, clenching her teeth hard in nervousness.

"Claire, will you…"

Her thoughts became dizzying, imagining Lucas as the father of her baby someday. Him tickling their little one's tummy with big green monster hands he found at Hasting's. Carrying him on his shoulders, with matching black capes tied around both of their necks. Would a monster-loving thirty-year-old be ready for marriage and parenthood? Claire wasn't ready, no matter how mature she was for the both of them.

"Will you…" He opened the box, revealing a bright, gleaming… movie ticket, "go to *Dracula Versus The Wolfman* with me? When you come back home, of course." A cheesy-adorable grin sprang across his face.

Claire sighed, and her whole being seemed to exhale too. "I thought—I thought you were, you know."

"Proposing?" he said. "No. You already said no to seventeen requests to be my girlfriend. Will you be my girlfriend?"

"No," shot out of her mouth without thinking.

"There you go." He smiled good-naturedly. "Eighteen times."

"It's just, you know about how things ended with Jack, and so recently." She gently touched his tan arm.

"Yes, he's crazy," Lucas said, squinting his hazel eyes. "Letting you go, and then coming crawling back once you open a hotel. Is he still calling you?"

"I only got a few calls. Nothing for a couple days now."

"Good. Otherwise, you should tell him he's creepy, stalking you like that." He paused, looking like a light switched on in his mind. "Oh, I'm not stalking you. Like Bob here, I'm in town."

The Kanes eyed him incredulously.

"You two are gorgeous ladies, so I can understand the skepticism," he said, "but I'm on vacation too."

"On this cruise?" Claire ventured.

"No, I'm going to Dracula's castle."

Dropping her jaw in realization, Claire nodded. "Of course. That place you told me about down off the coast a ways, in a little town."

"Yes. Where everything to do with the castle and character is based strictly off the book." He rubbed his hands together. "It's going to be amazing."

"Yeah, let me know how it goes. Maybe I'll check it out someday," Claire said. "Oh, and about the movie—

it's a date."

"Yes! So, this means you're coming home single. You're not going to like run off with some hunky cruise-ship dancer?" He tucked the ticket back into his pants.

"No," Claire said with a broad smile and laughter. "I'll be coming back home."

"Okay, then it's a date. I better let you go before the ramp ascends."

This time Claire went in for the kiss. Upon separating, she told him, "See you later, date."

Lucas and Bob waved the ladies goodbye, and the Kanes were finally taking a walk up to their ship.

"We haven't even sailed away yet," Zoey said, "and things are already off to an adventurous start."

The Sunburst was even larger than the mother and daughter had imagined. With sleek lines, hundreds of glistening windows, and colored flags lining the bow, it promised luxurious adventures ahead.

"Mother, watch out for rolling your luggage onto people's ankles," Claire warned.

"Uh huh," Zoey said, but her focus was taken away by the scenery. She romanticized the sea, down to its pungent, fishy smell. It was all part of its mystical marine allure. The latest romance novel she read was about a bare-chested captain who could swing from sail to sail, holding on to a rope with one arm and a damsel in distress in the other. *Perhaps I could experience something similar on this voyage*, she mused.

"Oh! Ow!" protested a fellow passenger, scowling.

"Oops! Sorry, sir. So sorry!" Zoey snapped out of it,

pulling her leopard suitcases tighter alongside her own feet.

"What did I tell you about ankles, Mom?" Claire was carefully wheeling her three black suitcases.

All around were wealthy, mostly older, vacationers. Claire didn't think to ask her mother why neither of them had opted for luggage delivery to their suite. Maybe because they didn't quite feel like they belonged to such a pampered class. It was just happenstance that the two came upon riches. Still, they expected to have a lot of fun taking advantage of their *nouveau* wealth. It was time for a much-needed holiday.

Zoey wore a sheer blouse over a tank-top, her long strawberry-blond hair braided down her back. Claire had donned a cherry-red summer dress, her dark shoulder-length hair up in a sleek French twist.

"I fear we didn't dress well enough for the occasion," Zoey finally said, taking in all the hundred-dollar sunglasses and thousand-dollar handbags.

"I'm just amazed we can out-dress them if we desire," Claire said. "But that doesn't matter anyway. We have our dressier clothes for later, not to be wasted on moments like this."

"I suppose you're right, but I do wish I had brought my lovely ruby ring for tonight," Zoey said. Then she spotted a group of older women all wearing red hats, complemented with purple fringe, feathers, scarves, or lace. "It's the Red Hat Society!"

"Oh, I think I've heard of them," Claire said. "Seniors who wear red hats and enjoy leisure activities.

See? There are more over there."

"Yes, yes. Oh, and there must be the Pink Hat Society." Zoey pointed. Younger women with pink hats were interwoven with the party of red hats. "Do you think I could fit in with them, dear?"

"Who?! The *Pink* Hats? Don't even try." Claire was serious. "I would like this cruise to be mostly about us. We have not had fun and relaxation in a long time. Let's just stick together."

"I know." Zoey would have put her arm around her daughter, in a side-squeeze, if they weren't continuing up the never-ending ramp. "How do you think Lucas and Bob will do without us?"

"I think they will be all right."

After finally entering the center, the Grand Foyer of the ship, they made their way to an elevator of mostly windows, decorated with twinkling lights. They exited on the top deck, where the most elite staterooms resided.

Zoey gasped. "That hallway looks to be about a mile to the left and a mile to the right."

"Oh, no worries." Claire quickly saw that their stateroom was not too far off. "It's just right up there."

"Oh, good."

Zoey had the key card, and she unlocked their door. The inside didn't disappoint. It was comparable to a five-star hotel suite in Vegas. A chandelier was right in the center of an exquisite sitting room. Champagne and cider in an ice bucket greeted them next to fresh-cut orchids in a vase on a glass coffee table. Two bedrooms off opposite sides from it had king-size beds, large flat screen TV's, and walk-in showers.

"This definitely is a celebrity cruise line. I've never seen such rooms aboard other ships," Claire noted.

"Wow!" Zoey exclaimed. "I still have a poverty appreciation for this kind of grandeur."

They opened a sliding glass door and stepped onto their balcony. They stood there, leaning their forearms against the railing in awe for a moment, looking out across the dark, rippling sea.

"There's the lifeboat," Claire said, nodding just left of the balcony.

"That makes me feel better," her mother said with a chuckle.

After hanging up several evening gowns and setting out dozens of high heels, an announcement in a Russian accent came over their intercom. "This is your captain, Vladimir. Welcome and thank you for choosing The Ocean Elite Cruise Line for your vacation experience. In one hour, 5 p.m., we ask all to gather for a mandatory life jacket try-on with an accompanying tour of exits and lifeboats. We will sail away in two-and-a-half hours— 6:30 p.m. I invite you to the traditional sailing away ceremony out on the Galaxy Deck. The Sunburst will be sailing to Kinikiwiki Island and arriving at this beautiful destination by morning. Bon Voyage!"

They felt thrills of excitement course through them upon hearing the announcement of the island getaway. They met back in the sitting room upon the captain's last words, all dressed for the evening.

Claire's large gold locket adorned her black satin

dress. Her hair was still up but tightened into a neater twist with a bit of bangs falling across her perfect forehead.

"Oh, you look wonderful," said Zoey as she centered her daughter's locket clasp more perfectly to the back of her neck.

"*We* look wonderful." Claire beamed. "Wow, your garnet red dress is to die for!"

"Yes, I thought it would make a statement. I bought it in the city last weekend. What kind of a statement does it make, dear? Nothing rude, I hope."

"You and it go well together. Don't worry," assured her daughter with a critical eye. "Why don't we walk around a bit before the night wears on?"

"Count me in," Zoey chimed.

They both rushed to grab their evening handbags. Zoey felt the doorknob to make sure it was locked on the way out.

Suddenly the door to the suite across from them opened up. Oout stepped a thin, happy woman, wearing a cocktail hat, a geranium-red dress to match, and a deep purple boa. "Oooh, your dress is to die for!" she exclaimed to Zoey.

"That's what my daughter said." She chuckled, happy for receiving the remark twice.

"Well, it is." She gleamed, her fluffy white hair poking out from under the hat. Her blue eyes were sincerely kind, and her cheekbones were round like apples. "Hi, my name is Kathryn."

Zoey shook hands first. "My name is Zoey Kane,

and this is my daughter, Claire Kane. You can call me Zo."

"How do you do?" said Claire.

"Oh, splendid. I'm here with a bunch of lady friends, but you know it is so neat to see a mother and daughter close like you two. You aren't in business together, are you?"

"Well, not really," Zoey answered. "We did have a very successful hotel." She didn't fear to brag. "But now we are looking into other options. Claire was an editor to *Eye Witness Magazine*," she added to top it off with a cherry.

"*Eye Witness Magazine*? Oh yes, I have heard of it, although I haven't read an issue myself." Her smile continued. "Oh, well, speaking of publishing…" She quieted her voice and stepped a little closer to the two. "I hear that Felix Belmont, publisher of *American Citizen*, has a room right next to you!" She gestured.

"Really?!" the Kanes said in unison.

"Yes!" Kathryn nodded vigorously. "Maybe you will run into each other during the week. Exchange info."

"Oh, that would be excellent." Claire thanked her for that bit of information.

"Well, see you, ladies, around. I have got a meeting to attend." She waved. "And I'm late!"

"Bye!" Zoey said, admiring her charm.

"Did you hear that? Felix Belmont is next door to us. This vacation seems to only get better and better, and we've hardly arrived aboard ship, Mother."

TWO

"Now take your life jacket and slip it over the head, like so." A crew member demonstrated effortlessly.

Large crowds gathered in separately appointed areas, learning how to save themselves in case of emergency. The Starlight Room, a large theater, was Zoey and Claire's appointed meet-up place.

Claire slipped her life jacket on within a couple seconds. Somehow, Zoey got hers caught on her pretty hair ornaments. Her arms were stuck upwards, and she looked like a crab to her daughter. Claire was trying to be sympathetic, while at the same time unsuccessfully resisting laughter.

"Help," Zoey squeaked, her enchanting brown eyes peek-a-booing through the front slats of the jacket.

Claire quickly helped by pushing down on the life jacket and moving her mother's hair strategically out of the way. The scene caught the attention of several people nearby, who tittered amongst themselves privately.

"This is not the first impression I wanted to make."

Zoey huffed. "Hurry!"

"I'm trying," Claire said, pushing harder, making Zoey hunch. Finally, the contraption pushed over her head, revealing a stressed, red face.

A crew member came over right away. "Ma'am..."

"Yes?" Zoey tried to keep her composure, fixing flyaway hairs.

"The adult life jackets are on that side of the foyer. You have a child's."

"A what? A child's? Are there any children on this ship?"

Suddenly she heard a baby cry and then spotted a little girl wearing heart sunglasses, teasing her younger sibling from a couple of tables away.

"Shouldn't they be on a Disney cruise line?"

"Mother!" Claire chastised.

"Just kidding. Just kidding. Sir, can you help me take this off?" Zoey asked the gentleman, kindly.

Later, at the sail away ceremony, Zoey and Claire had the very front and center spot at the railing of the ship.

"Oh, is that Joan Rivers?" Zoey pointed to someone on the deck above them.

"No, I don't think so. I think it's an impersonator— a lookalike. I bet we'll see many of them throughout the week."

"Ladies! Look this way!" A man with a camera

flashed a bright light, causing them to blink. "This photo can be picked up later on the Nova Deck. You will find them fastened to a wall of pictures."

The night air was chilling, but the excitement of their journey warmed the Kanes' spirits. It was completely dark out now, and the stars twinkled as a haven above The Sunburst. Zoey and Claire held on to the cold railing and looked ahead to the horizon.

Suddenly music played loud enough for the thousands of guests to hear from a speaker. It was swing dance music. People brought out glasses with wine to celebrate.

"How come we didn't think to bring a drink?" Claire asked.

"It's probably their hundredth time being on a cruise. They know all these things. We, on the other hand, have never been on a cruise. We know nothing." Zoey lowered her voice to a gruff whisper. "Which I think is abhorrently obvious to everyone!"

To that Claire didn't say anything, but smiled extra big. It was great just having the sea wind blowing across their cheeks. When the song was over, they heard a man's voice say over the system, "Are you ready to go to Kinikiwiki Island?"

"Yeah!" the crowd yelled back.

"I said, are you reeeeaaady?"

"Yeah!" everyone hollered louder.

To that, they heard the long low moan of the ship horn. Not once or twice, but five times, and then The Sunburst shifted and pressed forward in the water. And another song played.

Claire had signed them up for the 8 p.m. dinnertime. The two were seated and introduced to their "table mates"—a young couple on their honeymoon. She was dewy-eyed, having the porcelain skin that only a twenty-year-old can have. He looked like a football star. Both wore smiles, being polite and shy. They soon settled into eye gazing between each other, allowing private conversations between the Kanes.

"It's hard to keep from staring," said Zoey, who was a people-watcher anyway.

"Do you think we will see Mr. Belmont?" Claire asked. "I would love to talk with him. Maybe I could get a position with his magazine. I could write my articles from home and e-mail them in."

"Do you know what he looks like?"

"Not a clue." Claire pursed her lips.

An impeccably ironed and creased waiter took their order. Before leaving, he picked up the napkin Zoey had not yet placed in her lap and shook it open onto her lap.

Both enjoyed their lobster which was buttery, lemony and delicious. Dessert was on its way. Zoey settled on the banana cream pie, and Claire savored the New York cheesecake.

The honeymooning couple didn't touch their desserts, their mood suddenly changed. "But I already told you that I don't want to go on the caves tour," the young woman said, looking up at her husband with fear.

"I thought you wanted to swim with the dolphins."

"I still do, babe," he said in a smooth, reassuring tone. "We can do both, can't we?"

"No, not after what we heard."

"Nothing will happen. I'll be there." He caressed her cheek. "Besides, there's no such thing as zombies."

"Zombies?" Claire blurted, thinking about Penny's bizarre, though funny, excursions list.

The couple cast their sights away from each other and to the mother and daughter.

Claire quickly added, "I'm sorry for eavesdropping. I just—"

"It's okay," the young man said, resting a large arm behind his wife, on her chair. "It's nothing really. It's just rumors."

But his companion obviously didn't believe that. She crossed her thin arms in a huff and said, "It's not just rumor, there are actual legends about them."

"*Legend* is another word for *rumor*, babe." He gave her a soft smile.

"Don't treat me like I'm dumb. You always talk down to me."

"I do not." He shrugged. "I'm just more logical. You're more emotional."

The woman's eyes widened, lasering in on his like he was about to be dead meat. "What is that supposed to mean?"

Zoey shot Claire an uncomfortable glance. Not wanting a full-blown lover's quarrel to take place, she interjected, "Oh, it's quite all right. We sometimes can't help but be nosy. We have what's called Hyper-Curiosity Disorder." She laughed.

"Yes, I'm sorry," Claire said, setting a hand gently on the table. "Please enjoy your desserts. You two make a beautiful couple."

"It shouldn't be *you* saying sorry," the woman hotly retorted. "It should be *him*."

Claire's cell phone started ringing in her clutch sequined purse. "One moment," she said sheepishly. The husband and wife continued with their argument, rising in angry tension as she peeked in at who'd be calling her at a time like this.

Jack. Her ex-boyfriend of more than two years. The man she'd barred from her life after he promptly dumped her over her losing an upscale New York job.

"Who is it?" Zoey nudged Claire, asking quietly.

With a monotone voice, Claire said, "The same person who keeps calling no matter how many times I ignore him."

"The tax man?"

"Noooo, Mother." Claire glared.

"I'm kidding. We already paid off Hillgate Manor's back taxes." Zoey smiled, patting her on the back. "Answer it."

"But I don't want to." Claire silenced the ringtone.

"He's not going to stop until you do." Her mother was right but now was *not* the time.

SPLASH! Their once sweet-appearing table-guest had thrown her glass of wine across her husband's face. "Mother was right about you," she declared and stomped off in a huff.

The wine continued dripping down the man's square jaw and onto his suit's dress shirt. His face was the epitome of shock.

Claire giggled nervously. "Mom, why don't we go to the magic show that's starting soon?"

THREE

The Kanes managed to get a table fairly close to the Starlight Room's stage. While waiting for the magic show, the emcee asked if there would be anyone willing to tell a good joke. Meanwhile, the drinks were being ordered and served to the tables: Pina Colada, Itch Witch, Sailor's Grog, Purple Whirligig (double rum and crème soda with a purple pinwheel). There were all kinds of fruit daiquiris with garnishes of cherries and limes next to umbrellas, fancy straws, and glittering swizzle sticks.

"There is Kathryn, Mom." Claire sipped on her piña colada.

"Yes," answered Zoey, looking toward three booths of Red Hat Ladies. "You know, I have never liked purple and red together, but they have done such a marvelous job of making themselves so cute in it. And they are all different from each other; not one is dressed the same."

"Here are some more coming in," Claire added after taking another coconut-creamy sip of her tropical drink.

The group called across to the others, laughing,

seeming to be friends to all.

The volunteer joke-teller was giving the punch line—"Hunchback, Hunchback!"

"I think he's talking about you and the life-jacket today, Mom."

"Never mind, dear."

The music struck up, and the announcer yelled energetically, "Here he is, Larrrrrry Potter!"

The magician leaped out onto the stage, twirling out his black cape as he spun to a bow. He removed his top hat and placed it on a stool. "Yes, that is my name. Welcome. Tonight, I am going to astound you by causing things and people—yes, people—to disappear from right before your very eyes, behind this curtained box here.

"But first, a rabbit! Where did the rabbit go? Where is my rabbit? See there? Gone! Not only did he disappear, but you didn't even see him in the first place."

The band played, and he added a dramatic, "Ta daaaaa!"

"We have with us tonight, right in this very room, a very notable man. I am sure you all have heard his name, or at least read his magazine, *American Citizen*. Before this show, he volunteered to disappear for us. Well, actually he volunteered Mrs. Belmont to disappear for us."

The crowd chuckled.

"There he is—Mr. Belmont!"

Belmont's booth was laughing it up as the spotlight beamed on him and his smiling wife.

"Did you see him, Claire?"

"Well, not really. The light was too bright and

22

washed out his features."

A rabbit ran up on stage and stopped in front of the magician. Larry Potter, seeing him, said, "Not now! It's too late. You're fired!"

It looked like the rabbit threw a silver dollar as it popped up from the stage.

"Oh, so that is what you've been doing." He picked up the dollar, polished it and stuck it into his pocket. Then he picked up the rabbit and looked him in his eyes. "All is forgiven. Can you get more of these? What do you mean you can, *if* I stake you fifty bucks?!"

He set the rabbit down, and as it was running off stage to a woman waiting to take him, Potter called after him, "And lay off the bourbon, you know it causes your feet to swell!"

The audience laughed and applauded.

"Wait!" The magician trotted over to the lady who was about to leave the stage. He reached into his pocket and removed his wallet and took out some bills. Potter lowered his voice a little, but the audience could still hear him. "Give these fifty dollars to the rabbit."

She hesitated, to which he replied, "Trust me."

Having returned to the spotlight, the show continued: "Good evening, everyone. As I said, I am Larry Potter, no relation to Harry. And although I do wear glasses, you will see I have blond hair, and I am in my thirties—by the way, very handsome and single… hint, hint." His eyes seemed to meet Claire's for a moment, and she blushed.

Zoey nudged her. "He was looking at you."

"Because everyone else in here needs the assistance of a *walker*..."

"And," he continued, "I would like to start tonight off with a trick—a classic card trick. Don't worry, I will have the cameras zoom in on me so you can see every suspenseful moment projected on the screens to the left and the right of me. Let's see..."

He started walking back and forth looking for his non-voluntary helper. "Who will I ask?"

Quickly he ran back to Claire with a deck of cards in one hand, while welcoming her to shake his other hand. "Hi, what is your name?"

"Claire." She smiled, a bit embarrassed.

"Claire," he repeated into his little microphone attached to his black vest. "*Mi amour,* Claire." He gazed longingly into her long-lashed, large brown eyes which entertained the crowd some more. "Pick a card, any card." He shuffled and fanned out the options.

Claire went to grab the third one from the right.

"Uh, not that one," he whispered loud enough for the crowd to hear and laugh.

She went to take another.

"Not that one either..."

Claire laughed and shook her head. Finally, she was able to pick one he would let her have.

"Now look at it and don't tell me what it is."

Claire put it close to her face and then buried it against her black dress.

"Was it the Queen of Hearts?" He raised his eyebrows flirtatiously.

"Yes!" she exclaimed and showed it to the camera.

The crowd clapped.

"I knew it. Let me ask you, Claire. Do you have any king in your life?"

"No!" Zoey called out, answering for her daughter.

"Mother!" Her eyes widened.

"Well then, thank you... and for being such a great *volunteer*, I have something for you." Larry put a hand behind his back, and it suddenly reappeared with a red rose.

As Claire went to take her flower, Larry grabbed her hand and kissed it, but in doing so lost grip of his deck of cards and they fell to the floor of the stage, all face up. The camera zoomed in, and the audience saw projected on the screens that every card was a Queen of Hearts.

"Oops," the magician said sheepishly, part of the act.

Larry continued with a new, unwrapped deck to perform many great classic magic tricks, and it soon neared the end of his show, where he said he had saved the best for last.

"Now, for the last magic trick, would the celebrity couple please come front and center. Felix Belmont and his lovely wife, Sharon, are going to join me on stage."

Everyone cheered exuberantly in anticipation, especially Claire, who suddenly felt nervous for no apparent reason. The spotlight went to their celebrity faces again, now projected on the screens. The dashing publisher with black hair, perfect teeth, and mustache stood with his gorgeous wife appearing at least fifteen—

if not twenty—years younger than him. She had chic, shoulder-length blond hair and a pale blue dress. Mr. Belmont kindly helped pull his wife's chair out and escorted her, walking between tables to the stage.

Once they were on stage, the couple waved to the crowd. Larry interrupted the continuously clapping attendees by saying, "I have to my left a six-foot-five-inch tall box. I am going to ask Mrs. Belmont to join me inside the box, and Mr. Belmont will lock it shut, so we can't get out. When he hears me say the magnificent magic words, which I told him secretly beforehand, he will open the box again, and Mrs. Belmont will have vanished away. Gone!" He turned to Mr. Belmont, saying, "I hope it won't be forever," and then tugged at his collar nervously.

The box wasn't very wide. First, Mrs. Belmont stepped inside. She pushed her body right up against the side wall of the box and then Larry entered. "Now close the door and lock it," he told Mr. Belmont, who quickly obeyed, shutting it and turning the key. Several seconds went by where the audience heard banging and shifting around from inside.

Mr. Belmont looked at his watch, making fun of how much time it was taking.

"Okay," everyone heard from Larry inside on his microphone. "Shlama-lama-bing-bong!"

Mr. Belmont put the key back into the lock and opened the door. To the audience's surprise, Mrs. Belmont had indeed disappeared, and for added entertainment, the cameras zoomed in on Larry, whose hair was now mussed up, his glasses crooked on his nose, and his white collar unbuttoned. Lipstick was also smeared across his mouth, neck, and shirt.

Seeing the upset look on Mr. Belmont's face, Larry quickly said, "Nothing happened. It's not how it looks!"

Mr. Belmont punched a fist against a hand in warning, and Larry took off running behind the curtains. Soon, Larry came back through the curtain pulling Mrs. Belmont by the hand. His hair was fixed, and he now had a clean, buttoned shirt on, everything back to normal. She, of course, was perfect as before.

The crowd cheered. Zoey whistled, and Claire sat back clapping in approval.

That was the end of the show. Larry thanked everyone for coming, and the lights went dim on the stage while the lights in the room brightened.

Fifteen minutes later, the music kicked up. A blonde bombshell danced her alluring way onto the stage in a glittering, slinky dress. "Hello!" she breathed.

"Well, if that isn't Marilyn, I don't know who is," exclaimed Zoey.

"Mother, what do you say we get some dessert to relax over and get ready to retire? We have a big day on the island tomorrow."

"Sounds like a plan."

They managed to walk through the crowd and get on an elevator up to their suite.

Once inside their room, the two kicked off their heels and sat on a luxurious black leather couch. Zoey grabbed for the TV remote while Claire grabbed the phone.

"Yes, room service?" Claire said. "We would like a slice of tiramisu cake and a slice of key lime pie. Yes, and put a cherry on both," she added, smiling. "Ten minutes? Thank you…"

Zoey switched the channels until it came to one dedicated to The Sunburst's daily and nightly activities. "This is the life, huh, daughter."

"Oh yeah…" Claire couldn't agree more, even though a chill prickled the back of her neck over the irrational thought of zombies.

FOUR

Claire couldn't wait to fall asleep so she could experience another fun day. She fluffed her pillows before hugging the down comforter, feeling blissful. But her thoughts became distracted when she suddenly heard the Belmonts enter their suite, followed by some loud bumping and thumping around. She sat up and placed an ear against the wall, trying to hear better.

Voices came across as muffles through the wall. Not one word was discernible. She could only make out the tone of the conversation. There were sharp, short sentences, quick and angry. Claire picked up her cell phone and read the time—1:17 a.m. Soon it was quiet again, and Claire started drifting…

In her dream, she felt something strange on her foot. It was a white dove, trying to hide its head under her big toe nail. It seemed perfectly reasonable. Then a loud pounding of drums started, disturbing the bird, and it flew away, disappointing Claire.

"Claire… Claire." Her mom entered her dream,

wearing a gold Cleopatra costume with the neckline dropping immodestly.

"No, you don't! You are not wearing that dress."

"What? Claire, wake up! Let's get going. We've got fun and food ahead of us today, and I want breakfast!"

Reality came zooming in as her eyelids fluttered open. She stretched and said, "Hurray, morning is here. Mom, you aren't planning on any Cleopatra costume for Halloween or New Year's, are you?"

"Heavens, no! I would want to go in the knickers and long coat of a colonial patriot. I rather fancy that tricorn hat. If I pull my hair back and band it, so it hangs down my back, I think that would be a stunning look."

"Thaaat's good." Claire was off to shower and get ready for the day.

Zoey called after her, "And your mother doesn't look good in a black wig!"

"I know." Claire giggled.

The captain came back on the intercom. "Good morning, guests. This is your captain, Vladimir, again. We made it to Kinikiwiki Island at approximately 6:30. The weather outside is a perfect seventy-two degrees with a light breeze. Have a lovely day of play on the island. We are staying the night, so stay on the island as late this evening as you wish. Please enjoy your day. And thank you again for choosing The Sunburst for your cruise getaway."

Although the captain was speaking happy words, his voice came across as dull and uninterested.

"It's probably his bedtime now," Zoey commented.

Finally, they were ready and were exiting their suite when Kathryn again came from her own suite.

"Hey, Kathryn!" Zoey smiled. "We saw you having fun last night."

"You bet. Did you get to talk to the Belmonts?"

"No, not yet," said Claire.

"Well, I don't think you could have had much of a conversation with them last night anyway. They were pretty well sloshed up in drinks when I last saw them. I left the lounge before them, ya know. I know my limit."

Zoey and Claire leaned forward, ready to hear more details.

"Glad to see you, girls, again, but I've got to run. I'm late. See you around." She hurried down the hallway.

"Well, I thought I heard them clankin' around last night," Claire remembered. "They must have been intoxicated, like Kathryn said."

"Well, I guess the best time for partying is aboard the ship," Zoey said. "No drinking and driving."

"Hm…" Claire nodded in agreement.

Zoey lifted a finger in thought. "And yet, the Belmonts seem like such an immaculate couple. I can't see them getting slap-silly drunk."

"That's what I was thinking." Claire shook her head. "Anyway, Mother, do you think I'll be able to meet Mr. Belmont today? I would really like to talk to him about my journalism experience, if not just to say hello the man face-to-face and get a handshake."

"I think you will at least get a handshake out of him during the trip."

"The odds are good." Claire tilted her head with her eyes narrowed in thought. "But maybe I should just wait outside his door until he gets out."

"Yeah right," Zoey said, then her eyes brightened. "But I have an idea!"

"What?!" Claire's eyes also brightened, in hope.

Zoey opened her purse and fumbled through the mess inside until she came upon a piece of paper and a pen.

"What are you thinking, Mother? Write him a note?"

"Precisely!"

"No, Mom!" Claire whispered loudly with embarrassment. "We aren't going to write him a letter. I'll just run into him by accident, like you said."

Zoey put the paper on the wall between the two doors and began to write.

"Please, Mom. I was kidding about waiting outside of his room." She tried to grab the pen, but Zoey moved and quickly finished.

"*I'm* writing him a letter, not you."

"But you are my mother, and that will look ridiculous and desperate. I'm begging you." Claire clenched her fists, pleading.

"How are you my daughter? You have really got to loosen up, my dear." Zoey folded the note in half.

Claire followed her mother to where she was about to slide it under Belmont's door. "At least tell me what it says."

"It says, 'Your neighbors in room 202, Zoey and

32

Claire Kane, are inviting you to a small midnight party in their stateroom. Hope to see you there!'" She quickly pushed it under the door.

"How silly," Claire said. "Do you think they'll actually come?" Her voice became serious with hope.

"You never know unless you ask." Zoey shrugged a shoulder.

"You said 'party.' Who else will be our guests?"

Just then a group of ladies in red hats came out of two other suites across from them, promptly followed by a group of young ladies wearing pink hats.

Zoey's root beer-brown eyes looked keenly at them. "Oh, ladies!" They turned to see her. "There's going to be a midnight party in our stateroom. You're all invited."

"Really?" They chirped and commented amongst themselves cheerfully.

"Are there going to be games?" one, most elderly, woman asked.

"Absolutely," Zoey said.

Claire's face became hot. She could barely look at the women.

"I hope to see you all tonight. Mr. Belmont and his wife are also invited, so they may show."

Their expressions deepened with interest. "Oooh…"

"Then we will definitely try to make it," one woman said.

Claire buried her head in her hands and stood behind her mother, her sleek brown hair covering her face completely.

"Oh, and if any of you see Kathryn from room 200, let her know she's invited, too!" Zoey added.

They thanked her and then quickly scurried off to go play shuffleboard on the deck.

"Oh my goodness," Claire exclaimed. "This has just become even more complicated."

"No, it hasn't." Zoey grabbed her hand to lead her along down the hall toward the elevators. "We will just order room service. Why have money if we don't use it?! All we have to do is figure out some games. I'm sure they've got some great shops on the ship and Kinikiwiki Island. Maybe we'll find something while we're shopping."

The two went down to the elevator to get a breakfast buffet to start their day on the island with lots of energy. Then they would go back to their stateroom, get their giant beach bags, bathing suits and matching straw-yellow sun hats for the island.

The two rented a golf cart, which was customary transportation on the island. Kinikiwiki was nothing like either of them had imagined, even though there were pictures at the customer service desk aboard the ship. It was very lush with greenery, accented by the white sand of the beach. They zipped around the curves of the narrow roads, feeling the wind in their loose hair. The volcanic mountain had the appearance of having aged into a tropical temple.

They soon spotted two waterfalls. One that was very tall looked like it was coming out of the mountain where they would have rather expected to see lava bubbling from, near the top. The two took in as much of the breathtaking scenery as they could, switching places as driver along the way, giving the other moments for drinking iced mango drinks.

"Mother, what do you say we take a dip in the bottom of the little waterfall?"

"Sure. And I can hardly wait for our snorkeling appointment tomorrow at three o'clock."

"How could we forget?" Claire said. "I am so excited to do that!"

"So am I!"

Claire turned toward the small waterfall. She stopped their cart, and they removed their wraparounds, revealing swimming suits. Zoey wore a black one-piece, sprinkled with a cherry pattern. Claire had on a mauve two piece.

The two both carefully pointed a toe into the water.

"Oh! I thought it would be cold," Claire said. "But this is actually warm."

Zoey smirked. "Probably warmed some way by that 'dormant' volcano there."

The temperature was perfect on the skin. Claire went down to submerge herself completely, feeling the water wrap around her hair and against her scalp. She opened her eyes for a moment, seeing her mom's feet touch bottom, where there were many pebbles among large stone-like rocks. She came back up, taking in a deep refreshing breath and slicked her straight wet hair off her face. "Let's swim a little."

"Oh, that's okay, dear. I don't want to get my hair wet." Zoey wrapped her hair up into a high, thick bun. "I want it to look nice for tonight's party. You know how difficult long hair can be. Yours was once long."

"Yeah, when I was in the sixth grade," Claire said. "Besides, it's still past my shoulders. Anyway, what are you going to do about snorkeling?"

"I have a special swim cap saved for that," Zoey said.

"Okay, and it can't be used now?"

"No." Zoey smiled.

Claire continued swimming in the rocky pool and even went right under the water that was falling like a ribbon into it. Zoey piddled around, walking in water that only went up to her chest.

It wasn't long before a couple with two children, about eight and ten, came into the pool, taking away the luxury of having the place to themselves.

Zoey looked at Claire. "It's more children from the cruise, who should be at home playing on their tricycles," she commented quietly.

"Mom, what has gotten into you? I was a child once."

"But I took you out to Chuck-E-Cheese's for fun, not an island resort."

"Mom…" She eyed her with that look that meant *Don't be ridiculous.*

The kids brought with them a football that they

could soak in the water to make it heavy and wet for some fun throwing. Zoey and Claire watched as the youngsters walked further and further apart from each other to catch the ball from more exciting distances. The parents sat on the rocks watching them play with smiles on their faces and a basket of goodies.

"Hi…" The parents waved to Zoey and Claire to acknowledge their presence.

"Hello," Claire said, and Zoey added, "Hi."

"Go long!" the older boy called out.

The younger one went right up next to the other side of the rocks, as far as he could go.

"I'm ready," the little one called.

His brother threw the ball with full force. It spun in the air. The little one jumped and missed as the ball was too high over his head.

"Oh no!" the mom called out as they all saw the ball go up and above some rocks and out of sight.

Claire looked at the boys' fallen faces. "It's okay. I'll get it," she said.

Zoey just stood there in the water, watching every moment of her daughter exiting the pool and climbing up some rocks.

Claire reached a plateau of dirt at the top. She was sure the football had flown up there in that direction, but could not see it on the very flat and exposed ground. She saw a rocky wall to the right, and shrugging her shoulders, she thought it might have gone behind there.

She walked toward the wall. Hearing some flirtatious laughter between a man and woman, she froze in her steps. She decided to slowly take a peek, just in case she could spot the football.

Claire saw the back of a woman with blond hair, wearing a white bikini and floral wrap-around. "No, you're so smart," she said in a syrupy voice.

They were holding each other, and they suddenly started to kiss. *Oh, dear,* Claire thought. *Should I be watching this? No. I just need to look on the ground for the ball.*

"You're just so perfect, darling. Who could resist?" the man said.

Claire listened in, her ears like radar dishes after that comment. She tried to see what the man looked like, but a large-leafed bush was spread in front of his face. She waited until he took a step, allowing her to finally see who he was. Her jaw dropped in surprise. Quietly, she walked back over to the edge of the rocks to wave her mother to come up and see.

"Did you find the football?" the father called out to Claire.

"No," she whispered, shaking her head and moving her arms. Honestly, the football could have been a cow patty at that moment, for all she cared.

"Where's our ball?" the boys called.

"Shh!" Claire put a finger up to her mouth.

"Where is it?!" they called again.

Zoey quickly got out of the water, seeing the urgency in Claire's movements and eyes.

"Where's our ball?" the older one asked again.

"It's gone forever," Zoey blurted out, upset at their obliviousness to her daughter's request to stay quiet. She then trotted toward the rocks to climb up.

"Hey," the little one said and started to cry.

"Oh, they were just asking," the father said.

"Oh, now Junior's crying," the mother added. "Come here, baby." She called him over.

Zoey huffed, speechless, then continued until she reached the top, where it leveled out.

"Come on, kids, let's go to the big waterfall," they heard the father add, loud enough for Claire and Zoey to hear.

Claire shook her head, and Zoey rolled her eyes and whispered, "What?"

She motioned quickly. "Just come here."

The two went to the rock wall and slowly peeked around it.

"What?" Zoey asked.

"It's Mr. Belmont." She pointed to some figures in the distance walking by what appeared to be a path. "They must have heard all of us and took off for privacy. He was with someone other than his wife."

"And you were being a Peeping Tim?"

"Peeping *Tom*?"

"Are you sure it wasn't his wife? Isn't that her same cut and color hair?"

"I'm sure. This woman was well-endowed."

"Dear, you saw Mrs. Belmont briefly on stage last night, and you think you are an expert on her cup size?"

Claire sighed. "Okay, maybe it could have been his wife, I don't know. If we see her tonight, then I will know for sure."

"Give it no thought, dear. I'm sure it was his wife. Come on, let's go find something good to eat and buy some games. We can just wear our beach shirts and dry as we go."

"Okay," Claire exhaled.

From the snorkel and swim excursion, Zoey and Claire went shopping in the "tourist trap" of the island. But they both agreed they loved tourist traps! The shops were filled with so many colorful crafts, clothes and jewelry that they could never get back home in Riverside. After that, they decided to attend a feast that included pit-barbecued ham with a sweet fruity glaze that fell apart in tender bits on their forks.

Claire got only mildly sunburned from their day of fun. Zoey was slathered up with SPF 100 sunblock to protect against damaging, wrinkle-promoting rays. The evening was comfortable outside in the soft, warm breath of the ever-so-slight breeze.

Claire was sipping the last of a coconut drink when big drums intruded on her thoughts with a rhythm that promised exotic excitement.

Sure enough, out leaped six lean men—lean except for one, who was broad-shouldered with a bit of a paunch. They were all tan and wearing loincloths. Arms swung aggressively from sturdy stances, and thighs and calves—that Zoey imagined bulged in strength from running up palm trees—kicked in warrior moves.

"Heeegh Huuu-ho!" they chanted.

Fiery spears, twirling like batons, were tossed to the contenders. *Thwang!* One of the warriors had thrown his flaming spear into the sand next to Zoey and Claire's table. The pole vibrated back and forth.

The bigger man strode, beating his chest with each step—kick-stamp, kick-stamp, kick-stamp. He then stopped in a straddle-squat in front of Zoey and Claire. "Hah!" His black striped face broadened with a wide smile of pearls for teeth. "Hello, ladies."

He looked at Zoey with eyes that looked like shiny black marbles and said, "Especially you, with hair like soft fire." He backed up, raising his fists above his head, accentuating a large ribcage while minimizing the paunch.

Younger native men ran from either side of the show with fire extinguishers. They smiled at the audience and doused the spear's flames. It got a chuckle.

"Good heavens!" Zoey exclaimed, having an amazed look in her eyes.

"Oh, you loved it, and you know it, Mom." Claire chewed on a bit of sweet pineapple. "I think we ought to go down to the water, take a little walk and look around."

"Okay, I'll leave the tip."

As the Kanes enjoyed the wet sand between their toes, having left their sandals safe from murmuring waves, they gazed out at the huge expanse of ocean and sky. "That moon is scary it is so large," Zoey said. "It looks like it's on a collision course with the Earth."

"I know," said Claire. "No need for a flashlight. It's

plenty bright."

"I'd love to find shells. Do you see any, sweetie?"

"I think, Mom, that these beaches are pretty well picked over. Consider all the thousands of tourists from everywhere."

Zoey continued in a little deeper. "There's always going to be kelp or seaweed of some kind."

"Why is it called sea *weed*? How does anyone know what are weeds or what are sea flowers?"

"I don't know, but I do have some seaweed—or sea flowers—wrapping around my ankles," Zoey said, walking back toward shore, to more shallow water, to get it off. A bloated hand emerged out of the water, like a ridged shark fin following her.

FIVE

Claire rushed over, having noticed the hand. "Mom! Mom, you are perfectly okay. I am right here with you."

"What is wrong with you, Claire? Of course, I am okay. Do I look like I'm having a stroke or something?" Zoey touched her face to feel if it was normal.

"No, not yet."

"Daughter, sometimes you can be so weird! I want to untangle this seaweed from my leg now."

"Okay, let me help you. Just move up a little more and don't... don't turn around. I need to see how to untwine you."

Zoey walked a little more forward. "This kelp has got quite a drag on it." She looked down and saw something that looked white in the moonlight, floating with the motion of the waves and tying itself around her right ankle. "Crapper! What is that, Claire?! It... it looks like hair. Clairrrre?"

"Now, Mom... just hold still."

"Clairrrre!" Her voice became a squeal.

"I almost got it all."

Zoey could feel the resisting tug of the body being

pulled back and forth by the ebb and flow of the waterfront. She wanted to look back down but didn't at the same time. If the body were to flip over, she would have to face it, and who knew how long they had been dead. Her daughter's fingers dug into her ankle as she worked to remove the tangle.

"There!" Claire exclaimed.

The last tendril was released, and Zoey took off in a leap and ran up on the beach. "Where's your phone?!"

"Already dialing," Claire answered.

"That body with the claw hand will float away!" Zoey called from a safe distance.

"I've got my foot standing on the hair."

The police pulled the body out of the water and Zoey, and Claire saw the blue face of Mrs. Belmont. Her eyelids were open, giving a deadpan stare, and a mean gash was across her hairline.

Zoey shivered, shaking off the creeps from being tangled up with a corpse.

"The last we saw her she was up on a hillside, talking with her husband," they told the police. "No, they weren't arguing. In fact, they seemed very sweet together."

Walking through the ship's casino to take an elevator to their cabin on the top deck, Zoey said, "There she is. Hi, Joan!"

"I told you she's a lookalike." Claire shook her head.

"That is what she wants you to believe. And who is that sitting next to her?"

"Where?" Claire looked across the many poker tables and slot machines.

"Right there. See him? Big ears, whiskers." She pointed toward a stool at a Wheel of Fortune game. "There, see the white hair?"

"Good one, Mom." Claire managed not to roll her yes. "I see the white hare. Is the bunny winning?"

"Why don't you ask Joan Rivers?!" Zoey teased.

"I'm going to ask the bunny if that really is Joan Rivers."

"Oh, now you're being ridiculous. Of course, it is."

Upon nearing their room, Claire stopped in front of the Belmonts' cabin. "Hear that?" she asked.

"What?" Zoey asked.

"Nothing. I think we beat Mr. Belmont back. His suite has a sense of no one in there." Claire reached up and gave the door a knock. "If he is here, I'm going to tell him we were the ones who discovered his wife and that we are sorry." With the first rap, the door moved open.

"Mr. Belmont?" she called.

"Push a little more on the door, Claire…"

It creaked as it opened. "No one?" She then looked up and down the hall. Still no one.

"All neat and clean," Zoey assessed as they walked inside, closing the door quietly behind them.

They stood in the middle of the sitting room for a moment, as if crippled by the fear of possibly getting caught, or perhaps catching someone else. They could see the bed was made in a bedroom to the left.

"Why are we in here? What were you expecting?" Claire asked.

"Blood! All over the place. If not that, then it was just an opportunity and a question. The husband is always a suspect first."

"We aren't going to get ourselves wrapped up in another mystery, are we?"

Her mother didn't answer. In her mind, she was already wrapped up in it.

Claire looked around while remaining in the one spot. Even the folds of the drapes were looked over. Something shiny caught her attention. She picked up a gold starfish earring and placed it on the coffee table. "We better get out of here," Claire urged.

"I know. That would be horribly embarrassing to get caught snooping. Let me just quick-check the restroom." Zoey headed around the corner.

"Hurry," Claire whispered.

"Aha!" she called upon entering.

"What is it?" Claire stepped cautiously in her heels. "Is it another body?"

Zoey popped her head out, waving a magazine. "Nope, just some gossip journal on the floor."

"And that is important, why?"

Zoey met her back in the sitting room, magazine still in hand. "Everything else is just impeccable. Why was this on the floor?"

"He likes to read while he does his business? I don't know. Let's go, Mother." She was feeling the gnawing pressure of worry.

"Okay, let's go." Zoey rolled it up and headed to the door.

"Hey, Mother, you can't take that! Leave it here."

"Oh, come on. If anything, housekeeping would be blamed, not us. Come on." She waved.

"Wait…" Claire's eyes fixed on a picture on a wall

in the bedroom. "That picture is tilted and hanging a bit low."

"Well…" Zoey spun in her sandals. "Go look!"

Claire glanced back and forth from her mother to the picture. She finally ran and hopped on her knees onto the bed, next to the wall. Zoey jogged over to see her daughter scoot the picture. Upon doing that, it fell off its nail and came to a crash between the bed and wall.

The two cringed.

"Oh no, Mother, what have I done?" She pulled it up, and the glass was shattered.

Zoey's mouth dropped. She pointed frantically. "There's a hole in the wall."

Claire looked up, and to her further horror, she did, in fact, see that there was a hole smashed into the wall. She dropped the picture back between the bed, and the two bumbled for the door.

They exhaled as they closed the door behind them. With a brush of their hands through their hair, they composed themselves as if nothing was out of the ordinary before entering their own suite. Inside, they grasped each other's shoulders and let out a silent scream.

The Kanes managed to lay out all the goodies, beverages and games for their party that night. They decided to continue the evening as planned, not wanting to draw attention to themselves, in case an investigation aboard ship—over what they now deemed to be murder—would ensue.

While they were pulling open the drapes so they could see the island lights, they heard the first knock on their door. It was Kathryn.

"Helloooo. I brought someone you know, I'm told."

"Remember me? Matilda Dread?" the lady in the pointy red hat said, all smiles.

"Of course I do. It's been a few years since college." Zoey gave a friendly hand shake.

The woman was still sweet-faced with unruly hair, like Zoey remembered, only now there were slight wrinkles around her eyes, and gray hair framed her forehead.

"I saw you at the magic show last night, and I was telling the girls, 'That has to be Zoey Kane!'"

More knocks brought more ladies and more laughter with irreverent comments and jokes.

"Oh, I guess you heard about the Belmonts?" Kathryn said. "Police have taped their suite door, so no one enters. They're investigating!"

"Really?" Zoey and Claire squeaked.

Claire pretended not to know for sure. "Uh, we heard his wife was missing…"

"I heard she had a fractured skull and bruises," another added.

"To think, you go on a cruise to get rid of all that kind of news, and then something like this. Do you have a cherry to go on top of this fudge?" asked a woman with dark hair and a purple boa over her shoulders.

"Do you think she was thrown off the ship or fell off an ocean cliff while hiking—hit her head and drowned?" The room was abuzz now with everyone chiming in.

"The husband did it!" called someone from the crowd.

"You don't know that, honey. They looked very happy to me," said the woman finding a cherry and adding sprinkles to some ice cream.

It was hard for Zoey to keep up with who was saying what, but the lady nearest her leaned into another and said, "Yeah, but these cruise ships are filled with all manner of espionage, hustlers, and murderers."

The other woman narrowed her eyes and replied, "Well, I know I'm looking at you a little more carefully."

"I have it on good authority that the moon was high and full and anyone being thrown off a ship would have been spotted immediately," Matilda interjected. "In fact, the moon that night had waxed its ultimate size and lit up the night like a spotlight, so she had to have died in the daylight."

"Just how do you know so much?" asked another.

"I know about moons, nights and days, from an old college professor of mine." Matilda shrugged.

"Reeeally?!" questioned the woman whose eyes were now slits.

"Yes, I think I remember him, Matilda. He is quite famous actually," Zoey added. "You've probably heard of him," she said to the other.

"And who would that be?" asked she who was contrary.

"Dumbledore!"

The old lady's eyes widened, and her mouth dropped open. "Uh, heh … heh heh heh." She leaned back into a full gut of laughter. "If you don't beat all! Here, let me fix you a banana split. You're crazy. I like you."

"Mother, may I see you over here?" Claire gestured with a finger.

Zoey came over to her.

"Are you having fun?"

"Absolutely. As much as I can, after what we've

experienced today."

"Speaking of murder…" said Matilda.

"No one is speaking of murder," interjected a petite woman in a red baseball cap.

"We are all thinking it. Now let me make my point. There are caves on that island that have a reputation of Night Walkers, a tribe of Koona Cannibals that run along the hills and come down into those caves with their victims."

"No way!" disputed the petite lady.

"*Way*, my dear, and you would be considered a tasty hors d'oeuvre with that hat as a cherry on top."

"Oh!" exclaimed Kathryn. "I heard that story. They come down out of the hills and mix with people, but they always have something about them that doesn't seem quite right."

"It wouldn't be somebody wearing purple with red? That just ain't right!" A red-sequined woman laughed, jingling the ice in her glass.

They continued their fun—gossiping, speculating, joking. They didn't even glance at the two card games Zoey had purchased from a shop.

"Well, ladies," Matilda finally said, standing up, "the casinos are just getting going good, and I think I will go on a man hunt."

"Good luck on that one." Somebody laughed. "You bring a love potion?"

"Maaaaaybe."

The other ladies made a dash for the door with her. "Thanks, it's been fun…" a couple of them remarked. They all had smiles as they departed.

The next morning, after a superb breakfast, Zoey and Claire were mostly over their jitters. Curiosity started to take over, so the two decided to go back to the beach and look around. For what, they weren't sure.

"All you need is some common divorce sense," Zoey said.

"Don't you mean horse sense?" Claire asked.

"Let's face it. If one has enough sense to know they're in a troubled relationship, enough to get out, that's all you need to figure out other crummy problems."

Claire laughed. "I guess you'd be the expert on that one."

After looking around the beach in the bright noonday sun, where the body of Mrs. Belmont had washed up, they decided it told them nothing.

"Look, Mom, down the beach. Aren't those the Koona 'Cannibal' Caves the ladies were telling us about? How far away are they?"

"I'm thinkin' maybe three miles. Give or take a couple of miles. The horizon is deceiving."

"Want to walk? What else do we have to do? I'm oiled, and you're slathered."

Zoey raised an arm and then lowered it toward the direction of the caves. "Walk on!"

As they approached the beachfront of the caves, Claire announced, "I once walked nine miles at Yosemite Park."

"Is that the one the ranger had to sit you down in the shade and give you water? Then give you a ride back?"

"You ruin a good story," Claire said flatly.

Zoey laughed, patting her on the back. "You are my hero, you know that."

Upon reaching the last of the caves, Zoey assessed, "Cave number one was smelly, cave number two was wet and drippy; this is the largest."

They entered the last cave. It was truly impressive, with a high ceiling, craggy walls of deep crevices, and rock formations.

"This is my kind of cave," Zoey admired. She knew there would be plenty of opportunity to search around nooks and crannies for interesting rocks and shells.

They spent quite some time combing it over, scrutinizing the walls, ultimately finding nothing to pocket and take home.

"Everyone likes this cave," said Claire. "Look at the footprints in the sand. There isn't one unstepped spot. The *Destination du Jour.*"

But on their way heading back out, something unexpected caught Zoey's eye. She hurried over and plucked up the small white thing. She brushed and blew sand off her discovery and remarked, "Oh boy, look what I found! I won a prize."

Claire hurried over, her curiosity piqued. "Whatcha got?"

"It's a brooch... a cameo. Kinda pretty. I think it's framed in real gold." Zoey showed her daughter the two-inch pin. "It's got a house with a well and words that say, 'Go The Second Mile.' This is nice, and it's mine now." Zoey looked around just to make sure there was no one looking for it.

A balding, swarthy man in glasses entered the cave, wearing swim trunks and a flowery island shirt.

"You weren't looking for this pin, were you?" Zoey asked. She walked forward and showed him the brooch.

He had a moment of surprise cross his face, and then an uneasy smile, before saying, "No, not my style."

He licked his lips and hurried out of the cave.

"Okay, it is official. It's my pin. How about you? Have you looked around enough?"

"I think so," Claire said, satisfied. "Let's go."

The two exited onto the beach. A group playing with a beach ball had hit it too far, and a couple of kids took off to retrieve it. Just beyond the waiting friends was someone strange, staring.

"Mom, don't be obvious," Claire said, "but look past the people with the beach ball to the man looking right at us."

SIX

Zoey looked over her shoulder, feigning adjusting a strap to her top. "Would you be talking about the islander with a blank stare?" she asked.

"Yep. He's the one."

"There are creepy people in the world," Zoey said. "Lots of them. But, I do have to admit he is one nasty-looking dude."

The two walked back the way they had come, turning and looking behind them, every once in a while. After they had spent some time shopping for souvenirs, they decided to get back onboard for a late buffet lunch.

"I want to go see if our pictures are ready," said Claire, munching on an eggplant salad. "Did you know that all these photographers with the different backgrounds—flags, ship, flowers, oceans, palm trees—are employed by the ship line? They ought to make some good money on that. Everyone wants pictures."

Zoey was going through her shopping bags, looking over her treasure of goodies. "I don't remember buying this," she said, pulling out a grass-woven doll. "I'll have to take this back. I didn't pay for it. I don't know who'd want it. It has no face."

"Hello, pretty ladies... one with soft flames for hair," a man said, his gaze focused on Zoey. He was broad in the shoulders, wearing a beige dress shirt, and carrying a food tray against his small paunch.

Claire recognized him immediately. "Oh, you are the fire dancer," she said.

"That would be me," he said. "I'm in a show here on the ship, too. No fire."

"Would you like to join us?" asked Zoey.

"Can't, but thank you." Ever-so-seriously he said, "I have to practice my twirls, leaps, and slides."

"What is your name," Zoey said with interest, "if we are going to be seeing you around?"

He smiled, showing his pearly teeth. "My name cannot be pronounced by tourists, so call me Butch. What are your names?"

"Zoey, and this is my daughter Claire."

"What have you there?" He set his try beside the pile of trinkets, and then picked up the grass doll.

"Souvenirs. That one I didn't buy; it just got mixed into the bag somewhere. I'm going to see if I can find the shop that has them and take it back."

"I've actually been looking for one of these. What say I give you ten bucks for it and you can pay the shop that has it."

"I think you are paying too much, but sure…"

"It is now mine, right?"

"Yes." She nodded.

Butch held the doll by the foot and began to unravel the woven grass. He then started chanting and touching the doll against each of Zoey's shoulders, until there was no more figure of the doll. The grass was in a heap of strings in his hand.

Claire was astonished. "That was a little bizarre, Butch."

"Believe me, that was very good luck for me to do that. I've got to go now." He picked up his tray and left.

"Why do I keep getting chills at the back of my neck?" asked Zoey. "This cruise is giving me the creeps."

"Me, too. That was just too, too weird. Let's go find the Red Hat Ladies and hide out in the middle of them tonight." Claire shuddered. "You can't date him, Mom. I think he's a Koona Cannibal."

"Why do cannibals have to be so cute?! Okay, but we have to pick up our pictures first."

The two strolled the eighth level of the atrium. Walkways connected the forward to the aft of the ship, offering a view down to the bottom deck, which hosted the customer service desk, casinos, and more stores.

What the Kanes enjoyed most about the eighth deck was looking over the guests' photographs. On walls and photo boards, pictures by the many different vendors were displayed for purchase. Cashiers were conveniently stationed nearby.

"I feel like I have met everyone, having looked over all these pictures along the way," Claire noted.

"Hey, there's us at the Sail Away Deck Party!" Zoey placed a red fingernail against the photo—Zoey's eyes were closed with her mouth agape; Claire's eyes were squinting, and she looked as if she was about to sneeze.

"Nice!" Claire snatched it and hid it behind photos of others.

"Good idea. I would hate for Butch to see that one."

"Mother, what did I just say about him?"

"Yeah, yeah…"

They laughed, strolling to the next photo board.

"And look! There's one of Marilyn." Claire pointed.

"Pretty darn good, except didn't the real Monroe have blue eyes? This one has brown eyes."

"I didn't catch that. Good one, Mom. Wait! Wait a minute…" She pulled the picture out of its slot.

"What?"

"Look at those earrings." She lowered her voice. "Gold starfish, just like the one I put on the coffee table from off Mr. Belmont's floor."

"That means Marilyn was in the Belmonts' room?"

They stood there speechless a moment, trying to make sense of it. "Oh my gosh! Maybe that was Marilyn with Mr. Belmont, Mom."

"On top of the waterfall?"

"Yes…"

"And for that matter, has anyone seen Mr. Belmont since then? We might have a love triangle murder."

Zoey raised her eyebrows. "Let's take this picture with us. Who do we get a hold of…?"

Claire considered, then said, "Customer Service!"

"Why didn't I think of that? I wonder if the President and the CIA know about Customer Service?!"

After a long line of people asking questions and trying to straighten out room problems, they finally reached a uniformed lady with an Italian accent. She was thoroughly entertained by the explanation Claire was giving for why she needed help to contact the right people about their hunch.

Claire thought the woman probably thought she was crazy and wouldn't have any idea of how to handle their issue, but Elsa immediately called Ship Security.

Security spoke to Claire and Zoey, asking questions, and telling them the picture and info would get given over to the island detectives who were handling the Belmont case.

Right when the discussion seemed to be ending, one asked, "How was it that you were in the Belmonts' room?"

"Woo, didn't see that one coming," exclaimed Claire, later.

"It's a good thing he accepted the door was open, and we were calling to Belmont to give him information. We didn't have to tell them that I stole a magazine from his bathroom and then you broke a picture, did we?" She batted her eyes in a look of innocence.

Claire laughed. "Well, your breaking down in tears in front of security—mistakenly taken as sympathy for the Belmonts—didn't hurt any."

"Did I look guilty?! Because I felt guilty!"

"You can relax. It's time we had some fun. Let's go to the dinner show and see what has become of our Marilyn entertainer. Maybe they've got her down at the police station."

The Starlight Room's stage was dramatic with its sparkling backdrop of curtains and soft music. People were already looking for seats. The Kanes ended up choosing a corner table looking down the length of the stage. Compared to other open seating, it afforded the best view. Zoey moved in first and gave Claire the outside part of the red, buttoned, and padded vinyl bench.

The ship began to rock in slow motion, side to side. The waiters took orders without the barest of a misstep. Claire ordered lobster and Zoey had turkey with dressing.

Their dinner soon arrived, artistically arranged on their plates. Claire's green beans were bundled and tied with an edible vegetable string. The turkey had cranberry zigzags across the white meat, with a bit of dark meat in the center. The dressing was neatly placed in a small ceramic container. Zoey added an onion soup; it was brought hot, with melted Swiss cheese on toasted cubes.

Claire set down her fork, furrowing her brow. "Mom, I feel like my brain is being pulled every time we rock one way or the other."

"Interesting phenomenon, isn't it? Oh, look, our Red Hat friends. Hi, ladies!"

Several hands went up in waves with giggles in return.

"Laaadies and Gentlemen," a thrilling voice of suspense announced through the loudspeakers, "It's time for our favorite magician, Larry Potter!" A big drum roll promised a spectacular entrance. When the curtains opened by five feet, the bunny was sitting quietly by himself in the middle of the stage, his nose twitching. Then a large Vaudeville hook was interjected from stage-right around the rabbit's haunches, and he was scooted off. He didn't even blink.

The curtains closed and there was another drum roll. The curtains re-opened to find the bunny there again, sitting quietly, staring at the audience. People laughed. This time Larry walked out in a black suit and red tie. He picked up the bunny and stroked his back, handing him to someone behind the curtain and whispering, "Get him a carrot... and fifty bucks!

"Hello, everyone. As some of you recall, I am Larry Potter. No relation to Harry. Yada yada yada... You can call me Larry the Great, as well. Tonight, I am selecting a brave person to enter into a special cabinet." The stagehand rolled it out, black with ornate gold hinges.

"This cabinet here is no ordinary cabinet; this has special qualities. It will take you just this side of the underworld where werewolves and ghosts exist side-by-side in a chilling, grasping world of the undead." His voice lowered to a menacing tone of warning. "All manner of horrible will confront you, and only the very bravest can survive the experience of the awful damned!" He breathed heavy as if exhausted with just the thought of it. "Now, who would like to be first?" he asked in a delighted tone.

"No one? How about you, in the little red hat and purple feathers?"

The dark-haired woman's friends began pushing her to get her to move. She finally walked up to the stage with a nervous laugh.

"Okay, we have our hero volunteer!" He handed her a writing pad and asked her to write her next of kin on it. "That's good enough," he said. "Your friends will take care of the rest for you."

They laughed.

The woman stepped in his magical box, and Larry shut the door. He pulled out a wand and said, "Mother's pie!" He turned to the audience and said out of the side of his mouth, "That was always a disaster."

The cabinet gyrated, then stopped, remaining motionless. He looked at his watch and said, "We better bring her back."

He called off stage, "Bring a gurney and an IV for this braaave woman."

After the gurney arrived by a stagehand, and the IV was rolled out hanging on a hook, Larry tapped the cabinet with his wand. It vibrated again. "Please, ladies and gentlemen, do not gasp or faint at what we are about to see." He pulled open the door, and there… sat the bunny with a red hat and feather boa across its neck.

"What are you doing here?" he angrily whispered. "You're supposed to be over at the twenty-one table in the casino. Remember? Joan Rivers is expecting you!"

The contrary rabbit hopped off stage-right.

Larry closed the door again and tapped the cabinet, saying, "Please come back. Please, please, please." Then he jerked open the cabinet door for all to see the smiling face of the lady, wearing her red hat and boa again. The audience applauded heartily, and everyone was smiling.

He turned to face the crowd with a wide smile. "Okay, now, who would like to be sawed in half?!"

The waiter stood before the Kanes. "Would either of you be ready for dessert? There is melted chocolate cake and hot apple pie."

Zoey chose the apple pie, and Claire, the melted chocolate cake.

"Ladies and gentlemen," Larry announced. "The Monroe Show has been cancelled for tonight. But another Bingo Extravaganza will begin in fifteen minutes. So, stick around." He then disappeared behind the curtain.

"Do you think the police nabbed her?" Zoey asked.

"Oh, look, Mom. There's Mr. Belmont." He was walking up an aisle of tables, heading out of the restaurant.

But Zoey was looking elsewhere, amused. "Claire dear, you have someone very interesting sitting next to you."

Claire looked over to her right and there sat the

bunny, staring at her and chewing. He was wearing a black satin bow tie. "He is so cute. Do you think he might bite?"

Larry peeked from behind the curtains, looking across the restaurant. "I don't see him anywhere," he quietly said to an unseen someone.

Claire raised her hand and waved it to get the attention of the magician. Instead, another man came out from behind the curtain and looked across the restaurant, spotting her. "There!" he was heard to say.

Soon Potter was approaching their table with smiles. "He is so independent," he said. The rabbit made his way along the table's bench, so he could pick him up at the other end.

"We so enjoyed your show," Claire said.

"Thank you." He moved a little sun-highlighted hair off his forehead. He wasn't wearing his stage glasses. "I'm having a little private party this evening. Would you two care to join us? It will be backstage at eleven p.m."

Claire just sat smiling. Zoey answered, "Thank you. We would love to attend."

"Great! Just go through that door over there. I'll be looking for you. Save a little room for more to eat— lobster and crab, already shelled. See you then." He bowed, turned and headed back with Zoey's and Claire's thanks following him.

"Gosh, he sure looks different without the glasses!" Claire remarked. "Cute."

"Honey, look carefully to your right. What do you see standing lined up with the other waiters in their black waistcoats?" Zoey looked down and adjusted her neckline to be inconspicuous.

Claire nonchalantly started to generally gaze around the room, until her eyes rested on a waiter who was not chatting with the rest but was staring with vacant black eyes at Zoey.

"Mom, want me to go beat him up?"

When the two looked back again, he was gone.

The ladies got up from the table and headed down the hall, joking about all the different things they would do to him if they had the chance.

Back at their suite, the two were getting ready in their separate rooms for the after-party Larry had invited them to.

"I think I will be the lady in red tonight!" Claire called. "You ought to wear that gold and pink number, Mom!"

"Got it!" her mother called back. "Claire! Guess what I found in my purse?!"

Claire met her in the sitting room. "What?"

"Recognize this?" She held up a grass doll. "I haven't been to any shops where this could be bought. Butch destroyed the doll that I thought I had accidentally picked up. What does this tell you?"

"Oh, Mother. That stuff is only in the movies—a voodoo doll? Is that what you are thinking?"

"I don't believe in this stuff, either, but it tells me someone doesn't wish me well, so I'm going to be studying those around me. You watch, too."

"No doubt! Butch must have recognized that doll

he unraveled. So, the game's afoot, Sherlock."

"This makes me madder than blazes." Zoey had a determined look in her eyes.

SEVEN

Larry Potter had everything organized beautifully. An ice sculpture of a dolphin on a wave was the stage's centerpiece. Crab and shrimp cocktails were set out around it. He rubbed his hands together in what appeared to be anxiousness. He pulled up a sleeve to his suit to glance at his watch when suddenly the mother-daughter duo entered through the stage door.

The women paused a moment as if posing. They were taking in the scenery before continuing. Claire's sleek dark hair was pulled into an elegant twist at the back of her neck. She was wearing gold hoop earrings that matched a long gold-chained necklace—a medallion landing right at the bust of her shimmery red dress.

Zoey's pale pink draped dress, the style of a Greek goddess, was accessorized with one gold arm cuff and a large dinner ring. The sides of her hair were pinned with ornamental combs, causing a cascade of sensual strawberry blond locks.

Larry blinked a couple times and then exhaled.

"Pretty amazing, huh?!"

"Oh, hi, Butch. Yeah, their kind of flair is rare."

"Kind of like old Hollywood glam."

Larry turned his head and took a long look at Butch. "I didn't expect that sort of sensibility about you, Butch."

"There is a lot about me people don't expect. That's what I like. In fact, my native name means, *Unexpected man who reaches lofty places.*"

"And what would that be?"

"You can't pronounce it."

The Kanes walked in smooth, long strides in their direction. "Hey, Butch," Zoey said, stopping beside him. "I didn't *expect* you to be here!"

"See?" Butch remarked to Larry, then continued, "Remember, lady, I am a dancer. I have to feed my belly, and get some energy in me before you can watch me do some magnificent splits action on the stage tomorrow."

"Oh, you mean you are performing *on* the ship?"

"Yes, some dude broke his leg. The entertainment director of the ship called my agent this afternoon. Needed a replacement."

"Gives new meaning to 'break a leg.'" Zoey raised her eyebrows.

"Yes, Mother." Claire chuckled.

An orchestra from behind the back curtains started a melody. The ship took a hard roll to one side, causing Claire to stumble in her heels. She reached out, trying to balance herself, and landed in Larry's arms.

Butch commented, "Jeez if you liked the guy, I

could have just told him for you."

Larry smiled and used the opportunity to hug Claire. "I'm used to girls throwing themselves at me."

More guests arrived at the stage party. Larry had a few pieces of his magician's equipment lined against one side. Soon, there was standing room only.

People started to dance, and Larry said, "Claire, you are already in my arms. Let's take this opportunity to dance, shall we?"

That left Butch looking at Zoey and Zoey looking at Butch. They knew what was coming next. "Ask me," Zoey said.

"Okay, okay. Madame, would you care to dance with me?"

"I guess so…"

"That sounds convincing."

She giggled. "I didn't mean it like that. Excuse me. I would *love* to dance."

He struck a pose, holding a hand out to her elegantly, his feet apart. "Let's see if you can keep up."

"Well, there's a lot to me you don't know. I can head-bang, for instance. Ask my daughter."

Without a moment longer, Butch had her twirled around him like a helicopter's propeller. He let go of her, and she unwound round and round, sliding across the floor with the lean of the ship—toward Larry's large black, disappearing trick cabinet.

Zoey made contact. Thud! Clank. Clunk. The handle was knocked, and the door flew open. A woman leaped out of the cabinet, flinging her arms around

Zoey's shoulders.

People gasped and screamed out.

Zoey grabbed the woman by the arm, flipped her over and pressed her against the stage floor.

"You win!" Butch called out, rushing over. "Zo, don't move. Your opponent is a dead woman."

Zoey looked her in the woman's lifeless brown eyes. Her blond hair was matted with some blood, and the shine of the stage lights reflected a twinkle from one gold starfish earring.

"Mother, are you okay? Oh goodness, it's Marilyn!"

Butch said, "Zo, is now a bad time to ask you to an after-after-party?"

EIGHT

Zoey was back in her state room with Claire. The fall and fumble with the dead blonde had caused the back of her dress to rip. Her right ankle throbbed in pain.

"That was pretty freaky," Claire remarked. "I think we figured it out—a love triangle."

"Yes, I wonder what's up with Mr. Belmont lately. We haven't seen him around. We don't even know where he's staying since the police took over his suite."

"Maybe we should put it all behind us now. Forget about it. What do you think about dressing down for the rest of the night?" Claire asked, slumping into a chair. "We need to relax."

"You're probably right, as usual." Zoey sighed with a slight smile.

"Oh, what was that after-after-party Butch was talking about?" Claire placed a slender finger under her chin, looking up with amused curiosity. "Are you going?"

"It was a private party." Zoey sat with her daughter.

"Really, so I can't come?" Claire teased.

"Well, the private party consists of just him and me. But if you show up with Potter and sit one booth over, what's the harm?! What do I know of Butch, anyway? He had the nerve to laugh at the fact a dead woman tore my dress and sprained my ankle in a fight."

"Okay, see you later, because I am supposed to be meeting Larry in..." She looked at her watch. "Forty-five minutes." She went off and dressed in skinny gold pants and a draped gold top.

"Glad you dressed down!" her mother called out.

Soon Zoey left to meet Butch, making sure the card key was in her black evening purse. When the elevator had reached the eighth deck, however, it dawned on her that she had forgotten her lipstick. Back she went.

Zoey reached for the card, but the door was barely ajar. No one else was in the hallway. "I can be so spacey," she said under her breath, blaming herself. Heading into her bedroom, she gasped, startled by a shadowed figure in the darkness. She hadn't yet turned on the light.

"Where is the medallion?" His voice was a dry, coarse whisper.

"You smell dead," she uttered.

He stepped forward, revealing his deathly stare. "The medallion!"

"Okay..." Zoey's heart pounded, but she did all she

could to look cool and strong under pressure. "Move aside," she said, trying to think fast.

The man stepped to the side to allow Zoey to walk around him. She reached into her makeup bag that sat at her bedside table and pulled out the cameo she'd found at the Koona Caves. She held it out to him. "Now, will you get out?"

The man didn't answer. Instead, he took the pin and turned it over a couple times. "It's time for you to go now," he said in an even tone. He lifted a hand toward her neck.

It was fight or flight. Rage overtook Zoey. "Not on your tintype!" She grabbed her purse and pulled out the straw doll. "I suppose you are the one who has been slipping me these?!"

His eyes glazed over and his lips parted, exposing brown teeth.

"You're just kind of dry all over, aren't cha?! You got any spit in that hole for a mouth? Well, eat this!" She shoved the doll into his mouth, and he fell back against the wall in terror, his eyes wide.

The zombie-ish man spit it out, and his body convulsed. Zoey snatched the doll and made kiss gestures all over his face with it—"Smack, smack, smack, smack, smack!"

The man howled, stumbling to get to his feet. As he was running out of the room, Zoey slam-dunked the doll down the back of his shirt. He sounded like a wounded dog as he took off frantic down the hallway. In his haste, he dropped the medallion. Zoey jogged over and plucked it up fast. "Whew," she sighed in victory.

Feeling a little lightheaded over the unexpected scare, Zoey returned to her room and locked the deadlock, then called Room Service to report what had happened. Soon Security officers showed up, followed by Butch.

"I was just wondering what was keeping you," Butch said with animation. "I was expecting a problem, but not this kind."

"I want you to tell me what you know about these grass dolls since you seem to have a little ritual of unraveling them."

A long, low horn sounded off in the night.

"Okay, let's do it over a steak at our after-after-party."

"Yeah, that wouldn't be over a *stake* in the Koona Caves after-party, would it?"

Butch looked wounded. "You are suspecting me somewhere in this?"

"I think you are a believer." She narrowed her eyes.

"I admit to being superstitious and not taking any chances, like throwing salt over my shoulder for better luck, but that doesn't make it my religion."

She brushed it off. "Let's go to dinner, I am suddenly hungry."

"Good idea. My treat. Have *anything* you want."

"Oh, thanks." Zoey smiled, knowing dinners were free on the cruise.

As they sat together in a booth, Butch explained, "Some people absolutely believe voodoo is powerful, and these people suffer physical effects from it. In their minds, it is a reality. So, the man reacting like that is understandable."

"He needs to see a doctor." Zoey was making an understatement, remembering his smell and appearance.

Zoey felt fingers tap her shoulder and she jumped. It was Claire with Larry Potter in the booth behind them. "Did you hear the horn?" her daughter asked. "There was a man overboard."

"Yes, but I didn't know what it meant," Zoey said. "Really?"

The waiter brought Butch and Zoey's steaks. They each began a ritual of adding a dash of salt, then pepper, and finally a thick drizzle of steak sauce. "You're my kind of diner," Butch remarked.

"Tell me, Butch," Zoey said as she shoved a tender piece of meat into her mouth with much hunger, "what else do you know about the voodoo man? I saw a necklace of bones when I pulled open his shirt to stuff the doll down the back of his neck."

"Wow, you really did him in!" he answered around the juicy bite in his mouth. "First, you made him eat the curse that he meant for you with the doll. Then you gave him the kiss of death—in this case, multiplied by five. Right? I think that is what I heard you tell Security."

"Yes, that is right."

"Then, you made that curse ride him down the back of his shirt, meaning it would be coming within moments."

"Don't forget the bones necklace." Zoey took another bite.

"That… is a little more perplexing." He stopped and looked her in the eyes. "That would most likely be a ritual necklace of the Koona Cannibals. Human bones."

"Lovely! How do you know so much about them?"

"Live here, duh!"

"I suppose you've been dating their sisters and going to the Saturday night Koona dances," Zoey said glibly. "Look, I'm sorry. That was uncalled for. Forgive me?" She leaned over and kissed him on the cheek.

"You kissed me."

"Yes."

"You missed." He pointed to his mouth, nicely shaped, accentuated by smoldering eyes.

Zoey leaned in, and he gave her a soft kiss.

"Can you, by any chance, swing from sail to sail?" she asked.

"There are no sails on this ship." He smiled. "Why?"

"Never mind." She let out a little laugh.

Potter laughed from his booth. "Why don't you guys spin the A-1 bottle."

"Shhhhh. They are at a private party," Claire cautioned.

"Then I guess you and I ought to go dance." Larry slid out of the booth and offered his hand to Claire to join him.

"What is that?" Larry asked, and then sang,

"Heavenly shades of night are falling. It's twilight time…" They moved into an embrace on the dance floor.

Claire was coy. "You don't think we are going to kiss tonight, do you, like my mother and Butch?"

"Now why would I think that?" He winked and pulled Claire in a little closer.

It was around 3 a.m. by the time the mother and daughter finally went to bed. Their feet ached, and their backs too. It had been a long day and night, and they planned on sleeping in.

NINE

Claire was woken up by what she thought to be a foghorn. She stretched in her bed. Looking through to rumpled blankets in the other room, she realized her mother was already up.

Zoey walked over, her eyes red. She placed a tissue against her nose and blew.

"Ah, so you were the foghorn," Claire said. "You are sick?!"

"Yeah, but it is—*achoo!*—nothing."

"It doesn't sound like nothing. But I hope it is because I am looking forward to checking out the Koona Caves again. Check out this brochure I picked up at Customer Service yesterday!"

Zoey grabbed it and read, "The Koona Caves date back to prehistoric times. The local Koona Voodoo community used the caves anciently to hide from predators, dwell with their families, and congregate. Legend has it, the Koona Voodooists have roots in cannibalism. It has been said they crush human bones and mix them with their potions.

"Learn more about the Koona Caves and its rich history on a guided tour, each afternoon at 2 p.m." She handed the brochure back. "You get dressed. I'll go down and sign us up before the bus fills up, and then meet you for breakfast at our usual buffet."

Later, the two stood in the Koona Caves tour line. They followed behind the guide, boarding their bus with other vacationers. What they all wore in common were sunglasses, including a cute toddler girl whose glasses were pink and heart-shaped.

As they drove along, a buzz of conversations highlighted the drone of the motor, the screech of the airbrakes and the whine of acceleration.

"Well, did Larry kiss you, and was it *magical* or at least *great*?"

"Yes. It was a polite, quick kiss at my door."

"Phooey!"

"What kind of mother are you?!" Claire mocked with a smile.

"His philosophy must be, 'A kiss in time saves nine.'"

"A *stitch* in time…"

"Whatever! You are a sophisticated beauty. What real man wouldn't want a more meaningful kiss than that? Don't trust the man now. What's he got all bottled up?"

"Or, he is very sweet and doesn't want to make any mistakes with me."

"We are here, people. Get your cameras," announced the lady guide with black dyed hair graying at the roots and too red of a shirt with sleeves ending at the elbows. The bus rocked to a stop.

The tourists sounded like a cattle stampede as they clomped down the aisle and off to the beach.

As they all gathered into the last and largest cave, the guide stood on a little higher mound of sand to say, "As you can see, this is the largest of the caverns. The first one, as you discovered, smelled of rotting fish, because the tide washes in there and leaves fish and seaweed behind. That cave is the favorite of the crabs and shore birds.

"The second cave is too small for people, and I wouldn't want to go in there just on account of that. Whatever is in there has got to be slimy and threatening! Eeew." She grimaced.

"And then, this here…" She waved around to indicate the entire dimension. "Is the cave of legend. This is where all the infamous cannibalism and various voodoo rituals took place. This Koona sect was evil. Fortunately for Kinikiwiki, missionaries and the government came in and broke it all up. As a public warning, there were executions by hanging. Still, it is said that not all of it was cleared away, that there are still practices of sacrifice, voodoo rituals, and even cannibalism to this very day."

Everyone murmured, and some responded with

exclamations of deep concern.

"So," the guide went on to say with an unexpected smile, "I wouldn't be the last man out of here. Know what I mean?"

Nobody laughed.

"You can look around here by yourselves for twenty minutes and then we will head out to a beach café for some local color and then back to the ship."

Some people meandered around, while others went out to the beach.

"I think I will take a closer look at the walls and sandy little divots to this cave, Mom. There's something about this place. I'm drawn to it."

"Clever idea. Me, too."

About ten minutes had passed when there was some excitement from the front of the cave and then a scream. "Where is she?!"

Two men jogged into the cave, frantically looking around.

"Matty! Matty! Where are you? Come to Mommy!" A woman, red faced with tears, came running in after them.

"Matty—your little toddler, pink sunglasses, hearts?" asked Claire.

"Yes, I turned around, I didn't have her, and neither did her dad," she cried, working for all the composure she could muster.

Zoey and Claire began to search with the others, their hearts in their throats.

A long ten minutes later, Zoey heard Claire's voice

from a muffled distance. "Over here!" Everyone ran.

"Please, God," the mother pleaded as she ran to see.

Claire was looking down into the ground, which alarmed everyone once again. "She is okay. But she is in this hole and needs to be lifted out."

The hole was two-and-a-half feet taller than the toddler. One man reached down, lifting the little girl out. Her dress was dirty, but her sunglasses were still on.

The mother thanked everyone again and again. She walked away holding the child in a hug just short of a crush. Everyone was relieved, and their hearts began to slow down. There was some light laughter amidst the crowd, people releasing their nervousness, as they walked out of the cave toward the bus.

"Wait, Mom. Look at this." Claire was pointing into the hole.

Zoey looked down into the rocky, sandy hole. It was dark inside, making it hard to see anything.

"Look in against that wall of the hole. There. Here, let me shine my cell phone screen down there."

Then Zoey saw it. "Fingers!" Three gray digits protruded up through the sand. "Claire..."

TEN

"I know," Claire said with her phone ready. "Dialing!"

"Hi, ladies. Whatcha doing?"

"Butch!" said Zoey.

"I guess I'm too late for the tour."

Claire took a few steps away from them to report her finding.

Zoey shook her head. "You *live* here, and you haven't been on the tour, or do you know all the history better than the guide?"

"You expect too much of me, woman with soft fire hair."

"Take a look at that." She pointed down.

"What, did you find a big fighting crab? Oh, wow, Zo, an empty hole! Tourists are soooo easy to entertain."

"Take a little closer look down at the sand over there." Claire was finished with her call and flashed her cell phone's light down for better vision.

"Okay. I see a lot of dirty sand, big deal, and…

what? What is that? Fingers? Aghaaa!" He jumped back and almost fell. "Who *are* you, ladies? Everywhere you go there are bodies! Or in this case maybe parts of bodies! You guys are creeping me out!" He continued in a needy, wounded tone, "I will need some kisses all around my face, Zo, for comfort. But," he continued in a more resolute voice, "I'm not going in any dark corners with either of you!"

Two uniformed police soon came walking energetically toward their corner of the cave. "Someone found fingers?" they asked.

The guide called over, "The bus driver wants to leave!"

"I'll make a phone call, see to it that you can get back," volunteered Butch.

"Go on! The police want to write a report on this hole," announced Claire.

The guide nodded and turned to leave, seemingly satisfied. Although, she did raise her brows in alarm when more people in plastic coats, with a shovel and gloves, came walking from a government van.

"I'm glad they are going to fill that hole in so no one else falls into it," the guide muttered to herself. That is what she explained to the bus driver, and the people who overheard felt that was the responsible thing to do.

Butch, Zoey, and Claire stood around as observers after the police received a rundown about Matty, the hole, and how the fingers were discovered. One officer stopped the bus before it got out to the street to get on and ask the names of Matty, her mother and father, where they lived and their phone number. Everyone was impressed with how efficient the island police were about Matty's fall.

After some careful digging and picture-taking, one man in a full bodysuit and mask announced, "There's an arm and head attached to these fingers! We can presume this hole is a sandy grave for an entire body—standing up."

"I feel faint," Butch said dramatically, reaching a hand to his forehead.

"What?" Zoey looked him in the face.

"I can't help it if I am sensitive," remarked Butch, whose stockiness wouldn't hint at him being the type prone to fainting.

The police began taping the surroundings, including the front of the cave. It was indeed a crime scene. More pictures were taken all around. The three observers were asked not to walk around except when it was time to walk out.

"Okay, boys, let's pull him out." Two of the coroner's entourage dragged the limp body out from its hole. It looked entirely dusted in sand, including the face and hair.

"Mr. Belmont?!" Claire stepped closer for a better look.

"My word..." Zoey uttered.

"Oh, gross!" a voice came from behind.

Zoey turned. "Butch! I rather forgot you were here. Come on, let's go get you some lunch." The duo smirked at their big friend.

"Right… Powdered Belmont between ham and rye, chased by orange juice murder."

The three sat in a booth at a beachside restaurant, The Pirate's Galley. The girls ordered clam chowder with cob salad and fish and chips, while Butch opted for a double stack hamburger with dinner fries. Zoey, a people watcher, was delighted to discover that across the way and through a partition was Larry. He was standing beside a table of seated men of differing backgrounds. He was sliding something across to those she determined to be his audience for a magic trick.

Zoey nodded in Larry's direction for Claire to see. "Your boyfriend is having lunch here."

"Thanks, Mom. I will study his eating habits."

"Me, too." Butch took a huge bite of the burger, followed by an immediate stuffing of a fry into his mouth.

The girls gazed at Butch's chewing a moment and then returned to their own lunch, Claire giving a knowing smile to her mother.

"Who went overboard last night? Anyone know?" asked Zoey.

Claire shook her head while blowing on a spoon of chowder.

"Uh huh. This will make you feel better. It was the zombie guy. You don't have to worry about him anymore. He's a goner!" Butch took another big bite of the burger and stuffed a big fry, dipped in ketchup, into his mouth and then talked around it. "You know how we know it was him?"

Zoey replied, "How?"

"He had a grass doll stuffed down the back of his shirt and a bone necklace." He leaned back and laughed. "By the way, did you have to give the pin you said the guy took to the police?"

"No. He lost the loot, so the police were glad to give it back. I've got it here. Did you want to see it?"

"Sure." Butch took it and turned the pin over a couple of times. "This kind of jewelry has never wowed me... old-maidish, grandma type."

"Well, look who's here," Larry said, smiling.

One of the men from the table behind the partition had come with Larry—an Asian with a classy suit. "Hey, Butch! Nice seein' you here." The man put forward a hand for a shake, which was eagerly accepted. He had an accent, and Zoey wondered what nationality he was exactly.

"Mike! You gotta come and twirl some fire swords with me at my next gig," Butch said.

"Just might do that." A bit of a chuckle followed.

Zoey remarked, "We always come here for lunch when discovering murdered bodies."

"Oh, you guys still creeping out over Blondie in my disappearing cabinet?" Larry said. "Actually, her name was Janet. I think I've got to lose that part of my act for a while and get a new cabinet."

The magician picked up a salt shaker and napkin.

"Want to see a quick trick?"

"Sure!"

As he was placing the napkin over the shaker, Zoey had the sudden urge to cough. It was complicated from inhaling a bit of food. She hacked loudly into her hands, which was very embarrassing for her. To add to the humiliation, Claire knocked over her ice water in an attempt to reach a napkin. It made a horrible clatter with ice and water going everywhere.

Everyone reached for napkins and Larry tried to summon a server. Butch had to slide over fast or get his pants watered. Even the man with Larry was dabbing with napkins that were volunteered from a nearby table.

"I'm soooo sorry." Zoey continued coughing, but she was much better.

Soon there were a couple of servers with towels, and a tray for picking up left over ice. Some lunchers laughed once they saw there was no emergency.

"Well, dang! You know how to get attention!" Butch exclaimed to Zoey.

"Oh, come on, I'm the one who interrupted the meal," Larry protested.

"Sure, and I saw three guys stand up ready to give the redhead mouth-to-mouth!" Butch added.

Larry's friend excused himself, ending with a promise to get back to Butch with a call.

"Just so you all know," Larry warned, "I heard Customs is holding the ship further because some dead guy showed up in a cave somewhere and they think it is related to our ship somehow."

Then he said he needed to get to the ship and cautioned that it might not be that easy to get off again with all the investigation—something about terrorism. He quickly left.

"A dead guy in a cave, huh? That guy will make up any kind of story!" Butch pushed his plate back and began to move out of the booth. "You two are murder magnets, and yet so sweetly enticing, so thrilling and heart pounding, filled with scary adventure. It is terrifyingly interesting to be around you two. Goodbye, see you later. I have to go home now and cry like a little girl."

"Byyye, Buuutch," they said in unison.

"Claire, we might not be able to get off the ship if Customs is holding it because of terrorism. I wonder what has made them think that. They get information that we don't—uh oh. Where is it?"

"Where is what, Mom?"

"My brooch. It's not here."

Zoey moved plates, looking for it. Claire looked on the seat and under the table. After a careful search, Zoey concluded, "Somebody took it! Any one of the guys could have done it, including the friend of Larry, or the waiters."

"What is there about that pin that makes everyone want it?!" Claire asked. "Do you remember what it looked like? It had an island-looking house and a well, with the words 'Go the second mile.'"

"Yes, I can tell you every detail. I've looked it over well enough. Look it up on your phone's Internet. It looked like it could have been carved bone or shell."

Claire pulled out her cell phone and began typing and moving images on the screen. "So far there is nothing that is even remotely the same as that design."

"I want to go back to the cave again," said Zoey. "Everything happens in that cave. Well, except for the blondes. And yet one of them was found down in the ocean. It all seems to go back to the cave."

"We still have the afternoon. Let's you and I go back and look together, really analyze that place." Claire signaled for their server.

"The bill has been taken care of, including the tip, ma'am," the waiter said.

They asked the cabby to drop them off at the area where they'd gone down to the beach and found Mrs. Belmont. They would walk from there toward the Koona Caves.

"I don't know what we are looking for, sweetie, so look at everything."

"I've got my best smooth-ray sunglasses on, so nothing will escape my eyes, not even a can bobbing in the ocean."

As they walked toward the caves, they made a note of what people were wearing—or barely wearing—in the sun and swim get-ups. There were boats near and far, lots and lots of foot-printed sand, and as they got close to the caves, they heard insistent barks and snarls of a nearby dog.

"It sounds like a dog fight. It's coming from way up there." Claire started walking up a thin trail, to where a beach house was perched behind the top of the caves.

"What are you doing? Do you hear the *viciousness* in that dog's bark and growl?"

"I just want to make sure that there is no one in trouble."

As Claire stood at the top of the hill, she waved her mother up. "Mother, you have got to see this."

When Zoey reached the top, Claire was surprised that despite the dog's maniacal barks, her mother's eyes were fixed somewhere else. "What are you looking at?"

"That is the picture on my pin!"

The big, black, curly-haired dog was now in a frenzy behind a tall, rail fence. He couldn't quite push his head through, although he was trying. It pulled his eyelids back to slits as his teeth flashed, like a spiky bear-trap chomping and drooling at them.

The two walked up closer toward the property (and by extension, the dog). Zoey, when close enough, began to speak to the dog in a high, toddlerish tone. "Who's a cutie? Oh, yes, a little pooky-poo, babykins. You little cooty-cooty, sweetums!"

The dog stopped moving and snarling a moment to look at Zoey with disbelief. Then he took a couple of steps back and leaned forward again. Hair standing up on his back, he growled while gnashing his fangs, throwing spit.

The duo stood with hands on hips, looking at the

dog when he suddenly exploded into flames.

Zoey's mouth dropped open. "What the…?"

Neither one of them had found words yet as they looked at each other and then at the remains of the dog. Amidst the smoke and ash was a collar.

"Mom, you really ticked that dog off!"

"He did seem to have anger management problems," she agreed. Then she began to laugh.

Claire began to laugh, too, because of nervousness over the bizarre incident. "It's a shame Butch isn't here to see this."

The laughter grew in intensity, where it was hard for either of them to say their words.

"I don't think he could take any more, heee'd probably have a heart attack. Aghaha ha." They were wiping away tears and bending over in laugh-weakness.

"Should we… tell him?"

In an exceedingly high pitch, Zoey tried to master the answer, "Noooo," through a laugh.

Zoey wiped tears away with her wrists. "Okay, okay. We have to pull ourselves together and try to figure out what to do here."

Claire asked, feeling all shaken up, "Are we going to call the cops on this dog explosion?"

"I'm thinking, they aren't going to accept that the dog had a bad case of gas and blew up in a fart."

The two couldn't help it. They began to laugh again.

"You know I don't like that word, Mom."

Zoey continued, "They are going to begin to add up that we are at every violent occurrence; we might be hauled off. But, yes, call the police. Just tell them the truth about how we came up here. Don't say anything about the brooch and this house. We want to do a little surveillance ourselves."

"Surveillance?"

"We'll just follow along behind them. I know the police will try to find someone at home here to ask questions. We will just happen to be standing in the corner. Tee hee."

"Tee hee," Claire agreed.

A police officer came and took information, bagged the ashes and bits of a collar. He asked Zoey and Claire for a description of what had happened, and the two began to do a little giggling again.

A few minutes later, Zoey exclaimed to Claire in a whisper, "Well, that made us look like a couple of ghouls!"

The house was a cottage with paned windows and hewn stone going halfway up its exterior. The women watched from a respectful distance as the police officer knocked on the estate's heavy wood door. There was no answer. He talked on his shoulder radio to the local dispatch, asking for information on the house. A woman's voice broke through some fuzzy interference, saying, "That is the residence of a Mr. Felix Lee Belmont."

"Whoa… Mr. Belmont?" Claire said.

"Thanks, Lucy. Do you have a phone number with that address?"

Zoey elbowed Claire in excitement. Claire snatched her cell phone from her pocket, opened her Contacts file and typed every number carefully.

"If he's dead, who do we plan on talking to?" Claire said in a hushed tone.

"The man is wealthy. Maybe he has people taking care of the estate while he is away. That dog had to be fed by somebody."

"Good point, good point."

They watched further as the officer pulled out a phone from his pocket and made a call.

Zoey and Claire squished together, shoulder to shoulder, ear to ear, in excitement. The officer soon put his phone away and turned to walk back to his car. "Oh, you two ladies are still here."

"Yes, we want to make sure there are no more *hotdogs* on the premises," Zoey joked.

"Well, ladies, I think your job is done. You notified the police. You can go home now."

"Okay, okay." Zoey motioned Claire forward. They looked at each other knowingly. As they rounded a corner of the lot, they hid behind a bush, waiting for the cop car to zoom away. "We are not leaving here without seeing the inside of this place."

"For what? Why?" Claire asked.

"I've already trespassed into Belmont's stateroom aboard ship. I guess you can say I don't want to stop there. Come have fun with me."

"How do you suggest we get inside?"

"I haven't figured that part out yet."

The police car took off down the road. Just as they were about to come out from hiding, another car came up the road and parked in front of the cottage—a black sedan with tinted windows.

A man with black hair, wearing a suit, got out of the driver's seat, and started walking up the stone walkway.

"Do you recognize that man, Mom?"

"I think I do recognize him... Mike! The man that said hi to Butch at lunch."

Mike turned a key and went inside.

Zoey left her tropical blind and snuck up to peer into a window. Claire stayed put but panicked for her mother's sake. Zoey opened the door quietly once she saw that Mike had gone into another room. She tiptoed across the floor and unlatched the window. She returned, pulling the door gently shut.

"I don't like it when you take chances like that, Mom." They waited what seemed like an hour, sitting down, and whispering together. Finally, Mike came out, locked the door, got into his car, and drove away.

With some effort and Zoey bruising an elbow, they both got inside. The house seemed empty. It hadn't been swept or dusted in what looked like years. As they explored, they found a kitchen with rust stains on the sink and cracked linoleum. An entryway from the kitchen led to stairs going up and to another dusty, empty room on the left, which was probably at one time a bedroom. To the right was another bedroom, which was neatly clean, with a desk and cabinets. Looking around, they found maps with no marks on them, pencils, pens, a stapler—nothing at all unique. The files and cabinets were empty.

"This is not what I expected from a billionaire," Claire remarked.

"I agree. This place is not treated like the tropical island getaway that it could be."

Claire looked disappointed, then spotted something of interest. "Wait, Mom! Do you see how polished that one brass light switch is? Look at the rest—dirty, dull and unremarkable."

Zoey took that as an invitation to push it, top and bottom. No results.

"It looks like a dead end," she said, flicking the light plate with a fingernail as she stood thinking.

"The only thing out of the ordinary is the coincidence of Mike being here. Weird!" She gave one really exasperated hard flick against the switch plate with her nail, and it swung open. Behind it was a two-by-three inch indentation that had another push button. Claire pushed it. A portion of a wood-paneled wall opened like a door and revealed three shelves.

ELEVEN

The two looked at each other with smiles.

"What have we got here?" Zoey said.

"Ha! I know where your brooch is, Mom." Claire spotted it among other things on a shelf.

"Quick, let's take pictures with your phone of everything here. Don't touch anything unless you put it right back how it was."

Claire got busy, opening different documents, and taking pictures. On a spurt of excitement, Zoey took back the brooch, pinning it to the inside of her shirt. Before they left, they relocked the window they came through, and locked the front door from the inside and pulled it shut. Then Claire took pictures of the outside of the house and the grounds.

They were so glad to get back to their cabin aboard ship. Both took steamy showers and ordered their meals in. It was true what Larry had said: the captain came on the intercom and stated that Customs was not letting anyone off the ship and that there would be an extra party arranged on the main deck with dancing and entertainment the next day.

"At least we know one thing: one of the people at our table took my brooch. Who do you think it was, Claire?"

"I believe that it was Mike. He, after all, was the one who drove to the cottage with a *key*."

After the two enjoyed their dinner, they decided to browse through the shops. Then they would order tea and cookies and go through Claire's pictures. They looked at hats, jewelry, scarves, belts, candy, and artwork. A quartet was singing in a nearby lounge, adding ambiance to the fun.

Zoey rubbed her neck. "I'm going to go down to the medical station on the third deck and get something soothing for my throat. It's beginning to tickle like I'm due for more coughing."

"I'm getting tired, Mom. I think I'll buy this wallet and go back to the room for a nap before all the entertainment tonight."

"Okay, I'll see you there."

Zoey decided she'd better go to the restroom first. After finishing up, washing her hands, and then exiting, she stopped in the corridor of the men's room and ladies' room, squinting her eyes, peering past the deck of the ship and the shoreline. There was smoke wafting up from a spot on the island, and she was confident she could see some orange flames. She soon found her thoughts were distracted by an interesting conversation taking place in the men's room. They were talking in hushed tones, but she could hear well enough.

"Have you obtained the cameo pin yet?"

"No. This is getting out of control."

"You are going to arrange an accident and throw the two overboard."

"What if they are good swimmers?"

"Don't worry about it. People can get skull fractures falling from the ship."

"I'll make the call right now."

There was a pause, and then the man taking instruction gave instructions to whoever was on the other end of his call. "Yeah. Do 'im now... and? Yes."

The man resumed his conversation with the former. "He said, 'Don't worry about a thing. He's on his way.'"

Zoey didn't wait to hear what else would be said. She took off with her heart in her throat and adrenaline coursing through her blood. The elevators took too much time with people standing and waiting, so she ran up the four flights to her deck. Her heart felt like it was going to tear from straining and breathing hard. She had to get Claire and get out of there. If Claire weren't in the room yet, she would have to go looking for her.

Zoey slid her key card and pushed the cabin door open. There stood Mike. He was holding Claire's wrists behind her back, while his other arm was around her shoulder with a knife against her neck.

"Welcome, *Mommy*," said Mike. "You tell me where the pin is and I will let Claire go. Doesn't that sound reasonable? If you don't, I will slit her throat."

"Well, Mike." Zoey's heart was now in her throat as she quietly tried to control her breathing. "You have such a smooth, mellow tone to your voice. Too smooth, to be proposing a blood-dripping murder, don't you think?" She moved slowly and deliberately casual toward him. "I do have that pin. Why does everyone want it?"

"That," he said with a Cheshire smile, "is for me to know. Now hand it over!" His voice was now angry.

"Just a moment..."

"Give it to *me*," he growled, pressing the knife against Claire's skin. Claire looked at her mom with pleading eyes.

"So, if I give you my brooch, you will let us go?" Zoey knew that was not the plan, but the questions gave her time to move closer to him.

"Sure. All will be well. No harm done." His voice resumed to a mellow, almost musical, tone.

"Okay," Zoey said. "Look. Here it is."

She started unbuttoning her shirt to bra level and showed a flash of the pin. His eyes zoomed right in on it. Zoey feigned trying to unpin it, acting as if she could not turn the little clasp. "Could you undo it? I must be nervous."

He pushed Claire to the floor. "Stay, or I'll kill your mother!"

Mike stepped forward. With his eyes focused on the pin, Zoey took a quick step backward and then rocked forward with all her might, giving a straight blow to the temple with her fist and then an uppercut to the nose. Claire popped up, quickly putting an arm around his neck, tightening the squeeze with her other arm, giving Zoey the perfect opportunity to kicked him in the stomach. That doubled him over. Claire let go of him before he hit the floor.

Zoey said, "Stupid man! Don't ever come between a mother and her baby! The momma bears wouldn't go for it, and neither do I. Do you know what we are going to do? Throw you overboard, after we hit you over the head, and it will all look like an accident." She forced an evil laugh.

Mike strained to talk. "What? Are you nuts? You think you are so smart. There are two more assassins on this ship. You got a death warrant on you for tonight. You won't get away!"

"Yeah? Watch us! Come on, Mom!"

They entered the hallway and ran to the elevators. Ding! A bell went off, and after a couple of seconds that felt more like twenty, doors opened. An older couple was standing there, who looked a little surprised at seeing two ladies come in frantically pushing the "close doors" button. The door finally started to close, but not before a hand caught the door. It was Mike. He was about to enter with his knife, and the old couple screamed.

All of a sudden, their attacker burst into flames. "Agghhh!" he screamed.

Zoey pushed the button to the main deck.

Claire looked at the stunned couple and reached for the old guy's cane. "Excuse me." She pushed Mike out of the way of the elevator doors, and he fell into a heap.

The elevator kept going down until it dinged and the doors opened to the main deck, where a happy crowd was waiting to take the elevator up. Claire gave the cane back to the old gent and they got the fortitude to push their way out of the elevator.

"We've got to get off the ship, Claire. I actually heard the plot to kill us outside the men's room. There are people that we don't know and wouldn't recognize if we were standing next to them."

"Where should we go then and what should we do?"

"We have to stay out of sight." She pulled on her daughter's wrist, and the two trotted to a small alcove by the windows. It was out of the way and in the shadows.

"Let me look at your pin, Mom. I am still wondering why everyone wants it."

Zoey gave it to her and Claire began turning it over and over, trying to figure out its puzzle.

"This is crazy, Claire…"

"Yes. Yes, it is." She looked up from the pin. "Why is it that neither one of us is talking about a man blowing up into flames like the dog?"

"Oh, yeah, huh. Well, I think I'm glad he did burn."

"How did that happen?"

"Maybe his feet dragged too much against the carpet."

"You mean," Claire laughed, "he blew himself up when touching the metal elevator door?"

"Whatever it was, it saved our lives. And, well, I guess I take the weird as normal these days. It seems to be pretty much our lives, doesn't it? Does that make us superheroes, honey?" Zoey smiled over the moment of levity.

"Oh, definitely! I'm Wonder Claire. Who are you?"

"Butt Buster. You can call me Mom."

"Okay, B.B., we need to think what we are going to do."

They both were quiet, as different scenarios ran through their minds.

"Oh, oh. Look at this, Mom." It was dark out. Claire was holding the cameo up to the light from the ship's walkway outside the windows.

"Well, I'll be darned. It looks like there is extra detail if one looks through the cameo with light. There is a tunnel under the well, toward the Koona Caves.

They both looked through the window and over in the direction of the Koona Caves. "It's a fire!" Claire exclaimed.

"I saw it when it was just a bright light," said Zoey. "You know? I think that it is coming from the direction of the cottage by the well."

"Mr. Belmont's? It *is*!" concurred Claire. "We are in deep yogurt! I think the psychos who have been after us and murdered three people we know of, are trying to cover up their tracks. They know we know something. I only wish we knew what they think we know."

"Exactly. I think we can cross out the 'love triangle' as the motive."

In their seated window nook, Claire caught a glimpse of something that startled her. "Mom, act cool. I think I see a man staring at us from the deck."

Zoey shifted slightly, darting her eyes. "A creep with a bone necklace?"

Claire didn't look. "Yes, him."

"Come!" Zoey stood, grabbed her daughter by the wrist again, and took off running with her.

The two ran through the halls, knocking shoulders with strangers. Claire looked back. The man who appeared to be a native from the island, with dark tanned skin, had burst through a door to the inside of the ship, chasing them—his eyes deadpan, his top lip drawn up on one side from a freakish scar.

"He's following us!" Claire breathed.

Zoey didn't respond. She was too focused on getting away. Guests of the ship quickly moved to the sides of the aisle as they saw the women bounding down the halls.

"Should we scream?" Claire asked.

"Let's just get to our room."

A cleaning cart was rolled in front of them. They almost hit it. A nearby stairway brought more people into the intersection. A tattooed hand suddenly reached through the sea of people, grabbing Zoey by her hair. Claire grabbed a mop from the cart and whacked the man. His grip released and they veered down the stairs since there was no way through the crowd. That took them to the eighth deck of the atrium.

The killer followed and was now in a maze of picture boards and a throng of people. His eyes, deeply sunken in, carefully scanned the crowd, trying to catch sight of the mother and daughter. He walked through the crowd of customers who were studying their photos, some laughing and some smiling in satisfaction. When he finally looked down, he focused in on two pairs of pumps and sandaled feet, which could be seen through a space at the bottom of a picture board.

He put a hand down into a deep jacket pocket and took hold of the handle and trigger of a gun.

Zoey and Claire were standing still and silent, hardly breathing, when Claire pointed to the wall in front of them. There was a shadow of a man creeping toward them. The shadow moved a hand, pulling out what appeared to be the shadow of a gun.

He jumped around, gun pointed at the now empty corner. His targets had vanished. Blinking in rage, he pocketed his gun and trotted, merging with the crowd, looking again for the two.

It was a busy evening. People were either going to dinner or coming back, headed for a theater show. Zoey and Claire wound their way through the crowd as fast as they could.

Looking behind in nervousness, their eyes darted back and forth to see how close their assassin might be to shooting one of them. They spotted him about twenty feet back. Their hearts pounded against their chests.

They managed to wedge themselves into a filled elevator that was about to go up.

The elevator was stopping at every floor. The thought of their pursuer possibly being behind the door each time was a terror.

The elevator doors opened at the level just before their cabin's floor. A few people pushed their way out, and then a woman in a wheelchair was being sweetly accommodated. People moved tighter up against the walls of the elevator carriage. Helpers took their time, pushing, and pulling the wheelchair backward and forward, to line it up for exiting.

"Aaaaagh!" Claire screamed, shocking everyone to a pale standstill. She pushed her mother forward past the wheelchair and its entourage, out into the lobby. She followed, squeezing herself through and out.

"Sorry, Mom, that scream has been in me since the photo gallery. They just took too long on that last stop."

"Claire, honey. You poor sweetie!" But Zoey was just as full of adrenaline.

One woman was heard to say, "Well, I never!"

Claire responded as she and her mom headed for the stairs, "You mighta if you knew what we know!"

"What does she mean by that?" asked another woman in worry. "Never mind. Let me off! I don't like elevators anyway."

Half the passengers rushed out.

Zoey and Claire were finally at their home lobby when around a corner a big man stepped in front of them. "What's the hurry? Why are your eyes wild? What's happening, you two?" He took hold of Zoey, who wrenched herself free to continue running toward the hallway to their room.

"Get away, Butch!" Zoey commanded.

"Huh?" Butch looked confused.

"Get away from us, or you will be killed!" The women were running toward their cabin.

"What did I do? I don't kiss *that* bad," he yelled after them, jogging behind.

"Not from us. From the freak with the bone necklace, who is out to shoot us!" They kept running.

"Another freak?" Butch questioned, surprised. "Wait!" He quickened his steps to a run. "I want to die with you!"

"Yeah, he says that now, Claire, but wait till the first shot is fired. Then wee-wee-wee all the way home to Momma."

They were breathing heavily. Zoey had her key card out and was trying to insert it, but her hand was shaking too much.

Claire took it, inserted it, and opened the door. "You think they have Depends that big?"

"Ha ha ha. Good one!" Both of them slammed the door shut, Claire dead-bolting it.

"Let me in!" Butch started pounding on the door.

"Oh, crappers! Let him in," relented Zoey.

"Is a zombie making you say that Butch?" quizzed Claire.

"No one in sight. Wait! Help! Help!"

Claire quickly opened the door to help. Butch stepped in dusting his shirt off at one shoulder. "Hi, ladies," he said nonchalantly. He put his hands in his pockets and rocked from toes to heels as the two looked at him a second, dumbfounded.

Claire slammed the door, dead-bolted it, and the duo sprinted to the patio door—throwing it open and looking at the lifeboat that hung in the left corner.

Two shots came through the dead bolt.

Zoey and Claire climbed into the boat, with Butch scrambling from behind.

"What do we do?" Claire yelled.

"Pull handles and knobs until you get results!" answered Zoey. They yanked and pounded, pulling everything that even remotely resembled a button, level, or drop-rope.

Something worked, because the boat dropped suddenly and then eased on down the few stories of the ship, until it landed in the waves, sending Zoey sprawling.

The engine started up, and the two looked forward, seeing Butch seemed to know what he was doing. "Where to, ladies?"

"To the Koona Caves."

"What? Not there!"

"Claire, call 911 and tell them to meet us back at the well at Mr. Belmont's cottage."

"Mom, I don't have my phone. I lost it running."

"I'll call." Butch opened his phone and began punching in the numbers.

"You ought to get an up-to-date phone, Butch."

A shot was fired and then four more. Everyone ducked down. Then one more rang out. A man could be seen in the moonlight falling off the ship into the waters far below. Then nothing.

The boat bounded softly over the waves, with a bit of sea spray to the face. Everyone was silent, the lull of the engine and softly lapping waves the only sounds. The dark ocean, with its moonlit silver crests, was comforting.

The only thing moving within the boat was a pair of ears.

"What's that?" Claire pointed.

Butch turned and looked. "We have a stowaway."

It was the bunny. His ears flattened against his back.

Zoey smiled. "Are you running away from Larry the Great again? You look so dashing in your black bow tie with white polka dots."

He twitched his little pink nose.

"I'll take that as a *yes*, you are."

As they closed in on shore, the smoke from Belmont's shrouded the cliffs and caves. The ladies repositioned themselves, sitting next to each other along one side of the boat. Their hair blew back from the wind. Butch was silent as he stood at the helm, pulling a lever to slow down.

Claire put an arm around her mother. "We're going in, huh?"

"I've never been one to *completely* run away. Let's face the demon, which is a whole lot easier since we've called the police to meet us there."

A corner of Claire's mouth turned up in an anticipating smile.

Butch eased on the gas some more as they neared the shore, then suddenly jumped out into the three feet of water, pulling a rope, so the boat's bottom was against the sand. Zoey and Claire climbed out, stepping into the cold water. Claire grabbed the bunny before walking up the beach. Butch tied the rope around a large stone.

"Well, ladies…" He put his hands on his hips, going over to them. "Are you sure you want to enter the Koona Caves? We can always stop for a drink and just dance the night away."

"We're sure," the mother and daughter said resolutely.

"Okay, okay." He put his arms up in a surrendering stance. "Which cave? And what are you looking for anyway?" He narrowed his dark eyes.

"The one by the well," Claire said, "and we are not sure."

"As long as it isn't in the stinky one, 'cause that is where you two are on your own." He waved his hands to wipe the thought out of the air.

"Oh, why not?!" Zoey asked. "Just because it has a warning sign and no trespassing sign? Where's your testosterone?"

"Yeah," Claire added. "Just because we might reek of fish a week or two is no big deal."

"Mama!" Butch exclaimed. "Belmont's is burned down, girls. What could you possibly do up there?"

Zoey and Claire looked at each other, hesitant.

"Okay, you two need to tell me what is up before I go with you further. What do you know? What trouble are you getting me into?"

Zoey spoke. "The ship is on lockdown right now; voodoo dolls are hitching rides with me; there have been three murders thus far—Mrs. Belmont, Blondie and Mr. Belmont; hoodlums are trying to get a pin that I found; and crazed natives are chasing us, trying to make bone necklaces out of us. And then there is the fire…" She breathed in.

"In other words, Butch, we are in deep voodoo doodoo and need to solve the puzzle." Claire raised her brows. "Reminds me of a recent situation." She thought of mystery surrounding their home, Hillgate Manor.

"Well, you're right about crazed natives. I've been after your mother since I threw a flaming spear at her table in a *love* dance. Have you thought of just handing over the pin to the troublemakers?" Butch continued, "If that seems to be what they want?"

"Nah, I would rather be cursed, strangled by a zombie, chased, shot at, have dead people grab me, be in a fight with a man with a knife, and cause a dog and a man to spontaneously combust in a temper tantrum," Zoey affirmed, nodding.

"Besides, we're too deep into this mystery now," Claire said matter-of-factly. "We couldn't take ourselves out of it if we tried. If we just handed over the pin, I am sure we would be killed anyway."

"We would be killed! That's what I overheard."

Butch folded his arms, placing a finger over his lip in consternation. "Okay. Let me see this pin again."

Zoey pulled it out from under her shirt. She lifted it up toward the moon. The light shone through the iridescent brooch. "There is a tunnel that leads from the well down to the caves. And it says here, 'Go the second mile.'"

"We better go to Mr. Belmont's well then." He stuck the pin in his pocket. "I'll bring some of the extra rope from the boat, in case we need it."

Claire nodded. "Sounds good. I wish we had a flashlight."

"The boat should have one of those in its emergency box!" Butch said and started jogging back over to it. "And flares and other things we may need. Maybe some beef jerky!"

When he returned, he asked, "What makes you think the people who caused this fire, or the zombies, are not around? I mean, if you are right and this is a sinister, crazy ring of people?"

"Oooh, didn't think about that one." Zoey frowned. "Claire, be a good girl and wait for Mom in the boat."

"Hah! No way."

"Alright then. Let's go... Anyone see any red and blue flashing lights?"

"We have to get up the sandy hill a bit before we can tell that." Claire started walking while cuddling the bunny, stroking his back.

Finally, they were standing in front of the burned down cottage. Zoey wrinkled her nose. "I didn't know fires smelled this strong."

The cottage looked like matchsticks burned to the end. The stone chimney and stone elevation remained standing as a monument.

"No cops yet, Mom."

Butch began patting all his pockets. "Uh, ladies. I didn't actually complete that call. Remember all the shots fired and then the guy committed suicide with the last shot? It distracted me, and I really don't remember anything about my phone since then. I'll run back to the boat and look for it." He turned and trotted toward the boat, disappearing down the hill.

"Suicide? Like that other weirdo that cornered me in my room?" Zoey said. "Will the mayhem ever stop?"

"If they *were* suicides. And not the murdering of zombies who botched their assignments."

The bunny suddenly jumped out of Claire's arms and hopped over to the well. He made a final hop to the well's stone rim, looked down a moment and then leaped down into it.

"Well, *Alice*, I guess we better go over and see why the bunny went down the hole," said Zoey.

"We can't see down a hole at night without a flashlight, Mother. Where's Butch?"

112

They headed for the slope of the hill to see what was keeping him. When they looked down, they didn't see Butch… or the boat.

"What did I tell you? Wee-wee-wee. Of course, you know what this means—his lips can never touch mine."

"That'll teach him, Mom. Look, there's a flashlight on the ground, there." She pointed. "I'll get it."

When Claire got back up the hill, she complained, "I am so disappointed in Butch. But, at least he threw the flashlight onto the beach for us."

"Yeah, remind me to take it back to the ship when this is all over, so I can shine it in his face and spotlight him as a coward."

"I still want to look down the well. I don't see anyone to be afraid of, so let's not leave here until we see what is at the bottom."

They both were leaning into the well, the glow of the flashlight shining back on their faces in the dark.

"Okay, there's a metal ladder going down the side of the well's wall, all the way to the dry dirt floor. What say we climb down just to take a peek? If we don't think it is safe to go any further, we'll come back up and take a cab to the police station."

Claire's plan seemed reasonable to Zoey, so down they went, Claire leading with the flashlight.

When they reached the bottom, they peered further down into the tunnel, which amounted to hewn-out stone and dirt with wooden beams holding it all up.

"I guess it wouldn't hurt just to walk a little way down," Claire whispered.

"Okay," Zoey agreed. "I don't see any bunny. I wouldn't be surprised if he were the mastermind of all of these goings on."

They walked on without incident, so they continued on deeper, always ready to run, listening for any sound that would cause them to turn around. The tunnel suddenly took a turn. As the two came around the bend, they stood at the mouth of a dark cavern. "What do you want to do now, Mom?"

"Shall we shine a light in?"

Claire flashed the light in and saw that it was somewhat of a small arena. They entered carefully.

"Wow. I'm guessing a cave behind the caves." Claire moved her flashlight around the cavern and saw other tunnels leading off. As she turned with her light in the direction she came from, she was shocked to see two bare-skinned men with bone necklaces, loincloths, feather headdresses, tribal tattoos, and red-painted faces. "Mother, we have a situation."

Zoey turned around, and to her horror, the natives looked at her through vacant eyes.

TWELVE

She took Claire by the wrist and started backing up slowly. "Normally, the sight of bare-chested men would make me happy. Not right now. Run!"

They sprinted past the men, the light of the flashlight shaking along as they went.

"Turn out your flashlight and take my hand as we run for that opening," she whispered in Claire's ear.

The light went out, and they started running in the remembered direction around the zombie-looking men for the cave opening when—*pop-pop-pop*—lights went on around the cave walls. They were soon taken in the hands of the two huge men. Other men of the same appearance walked out from behind rock formations, which had previously concealed them. Zoey and Claire were brought to the middle of the arena.

There was a raised stone platform in front. Everyone stood silently, looking to it and waiting. Soon the white bunny with the polka dotted bow tie hopped up and sat down in the middle of it.

"See there, Claire? He is the ring leader, mastermind. Just like I suspected." None of the men moved a muscle and continued to stare directly ahead.

A figure in a gilded face mask plumed with colorful feathers came to the platform. He had long, black hair that was decorated with red beads. The bunny hopped away. The man, too, had a bone necklace, but also wore a more modest covering of a golden material around his waist. A follower handed him a staff with a lighted crystal globe. The staff itself was carved in a swirl to the bottom. He looked in the direction of the mother and daughter, and said in a deep, microphoned voice, "You may speak."

"You must be a techno-Koona of whom would be—cannibals?" asked Zoey.

"Mother…" Claire hoarsely whispered in distress.

The leader laughed. "You would be techno-cally right." He continued, "You have conveniently interrupted our meeting tonight, but you are welcome. In fact, you are invited to our feast. Ha ha ha. Bring two poles and bind them."

Two men ran forward with two round poles, six inches in width, and staked them into the middle of the dirt arena. Then Zoey and Claire were bound to them.

The figure raised his hand and pointed to the left. "Mr. D.J., would you provide us with inspirational music?"

Kettle drums began pulsing, and the men circled with their spears and lit them on fire. "We keep a little of the old tradition, Zoey and Claire."

"You know our names?" asked Claire.

"How could we not? You have been awful nuisances."

"Why didn't you eat Mr. Belmont?" called Zoey. "Aren't you behind the murders?"

A tribal man pointed a fiery spear at her throat. "Not so fast, Mr. Sergeant at Arms," said the leader. "Let us mind our manners. We have no reason to rush here." The leader continued, "There is evil all around. Even within well-dressed, affluent, educated people. Mr. Belmont was up to his fingertips in greed and warmongering. He was also a liar, who was pretending to still be financially stable. He got what he deserved."

"What about Mrs. Belmont?" Claire was now confident enough to ask.

"Mrs. Belmont? She was a victim of jealousy. Another woman, just as greedy as Belmont, murdered her. We had nothing to do with her. We only murder as needed. For instance, you have threatened our society's well-being by nosing around. We are a *secret* society."

"One more question."

"Yes, Mrs. Kane. By all means, a last request."

"What then is your main purpose in these caves? Secrecy and murder? There has to be a better reason than cannibalism. I don't know that I take you for being a standard Koona Cannibal."

"Very discerning. Oh, we are warmongers also. Except ours is as necessary. Mr. Belmont's reason was money—capitalism. Ours is for a better life. We would take down imperialistic nations and bring peace to the world."

"Peace by force," Zoey said. "Imagine that. How are you going to achieve that holed-up in caves?"

"Time to move on with the entertainment." The drums picked up again. He raised both arms and the men yelled together, "Ho!" and began to step-dance and chant around Zoey and Claire. Every so often the natives would all rush to a duo who held spears pointed at the women and then would rush backward to their larger circle.

A large ornate chair was brought for the chief to sit on. He was served a drink as he watched the evening's festivities. Pretty soon, it appeared the chief was nodding off, as his masked head would droop. A definite snore soon resounded out from his unseen microphone. The dancers continued their routine, closing in on the mother and daughter, then marching backward into their circle.

When the circle closed in the next time, one of the dancers pointed a red-hot spear tip at Zoey. He spoke in words that were not in sync with the chant but kept the beat to blend in. "When your ropes drop—run out the way—you came in. Ho! Wait for Claire's ropes—to drop. Hoooo hah!"

Zoey could see that Claire heard the same message because she gave a knowing look to the native. She could feel the heat of her rescuer's blade near her wrists. Seconds later, with the help of the same glowing hot blade, a loose part of Claire's ropes, behind her back, were burned and cut.

After one more circled approach, Zoey felt her ropes drop against her palms. She held on to them until Claire's hands were completely free.

With the next retreat of the natives into the larger ring, Zoey grabbed Claire. They ran between some of the chanters, who didn't even blink, and out of the arena.

But this time they had no flashlight, and Claire called back to her mom, "Take hold of the neck of my blouse. I'll keep a hand touching the wall, so we don't get lost."

Zoey listened. They only fell once. They got back up, reorganized, and took off again. Finally, they saw a pool of light from what had to be the moon shining down the well.

After reaching the top of the well, Claire made sure she helped her mother out. "I feel another scream, Mom."

Zoey began to cry. "Come on! I can cry and run, too. Let's get out of here."

As they ran, Zoey said, "All I could think about was watching my sweet daughter killed right before my eyes."

"Thank God we were helped. Nobody ran after us. How would you explain that? Where are we going?"

"Just keep running! It will come to us." About that time, Zoey could hear another set of feet running. As she turned to see what lunatic was behind her, the bunny whizzed on by them.

"He looks like he is late for a very important date. Follow him!"

The bunny stopped every once in a while, and looked back at them, taking time to chew a little cud. As soon as the girls would get close enough, he would take off again.

They were soon at a resort hotel called Sea Winds. It had thatched roofs, palm trees, and a pale-blue lighted swimming pool. Soft island music wafted through the eaves. The front doors automatically swished open, and on their way to the front desk, Claire swooped up their furry leader into her grasp.

The lady registrar in a green skirt-suit eyed Claire as the bunny was placed atop the reception desk. "We need a room," the tired guest said, smoothing down some flyaway hairs.

The registrar squinted behind narrow black-rimmed glasses at the sweaty and dirty women. "You have no luggage?" she asked.

"No," answered Claire.

"Identification or credit card?"

"Well—"

"...But you do have a rabbit who *is* dressed appropriately."

"True," acknowledged Claire, lifting a finger. "But—"

"I'm afraid the policy of this hotel does not allow for transients," the woman said, looking down over her glasses.

Zoey batted her eyelashes, managing to remain somewhat calm. "Please hand me the telephone, and I can clear up your concern immediately."

"We don't allow personal calls from the desk phones. There is a pay phone in the lobby there."

Zoey reached over the desk counter and picked up the phone, lifted the receiver, and punched in a phone number.

"Hi, Lew. This is Zoey Kane. Claire and I are standing at the reception desk of Sea Winds Resort Hotel. I wonder if you can vouch for us with the lady here because we don't have luggage or a purse... and our makeup and hair are a mess. And, we have a rabbit with us... Yes. You guessed correctly. You know us too well." Zoey laughed. "I will be calling the police. We are okay, thanks... Sure." She handed the phone to the astonished registrar. "He wants to talk to you."

"Hello? Yes, sir. Right away! Yes, I will. Yes. Yes." She hung up and motioned for the man standing down at a computer behind the counter. "Rod, please take Mrs. and Miss Kane to the top floor—the Island Sun suite." Looking at Zoey and Claire, she said, "You have carte blanche, compliments of Mr. Kipperman." Then addressing Rod again, she added, "Make sure the staff knows these are guests of Mr. Kipperman. And the rabbit gets whatever he wants."

"I would like to use the desk phone again," Zoey said.

"Yes, ma'am. I also apologize for the inconvenience I've caused you."

"Thank you. All is well."

After a moment of listening to ringing on the other end, a voice answered, "Detective Bennard speaking."

"Hello, Detective. This is Zoey Kane—vacationer. I have some important, distressing news to tell you. This must be immediate. Send as many police to Mr. Belmont's cottage above the Koona Caves. Enter the well there down a ladder. Then, follow the tunnel with weapons drawn, which will open into a cavern. There are about fifty tribesmen with spears. And a chief—he has admitted murder."

"How do you have all this information, Mrs. Kane?"

"Because we discovered the tunnel from the well, were bound and escaped with our lives. If you hurry, you can catch them all and have three murders solved, and I'm thinking two suicides as well."

"Mrs. Kane, I am dispatching police units now, and I will be personally over to see you for a report. Uh, where would that be?"

"We are at Sea Winds in the Island Sun suite."

"Very swank! I'll be there in approximately twenty…"

"Okay," Zoey hung up. "We are ready to go to our room. Where are the elevators…" She read the name on the woman's lapel pin. "Ms. Dobbs?"

"You will be taking that private elevator over in this corner here." She then nodded to Rod.

"This way please," he said, and the two followed him, where he entered a code to open the doors. "Here is your key card, which will also open these doors. The elevator takes you right to a small foyer to your door. This key card also opens your suite door. Any visitors will call you from the desk. We will open the elevator for them from there. Would you like me to accompany you?"

"No. We can take it from here, Rod. We are expecting Detective Bennard. Send him up, please. Also, send us up lobster dinners, a nice creamy soup, and mint herb tea. Send up four of all of those. Oh, don't forget bunny food and a cat box with litter."

"Yes, ma'am. May I ask if you are relatives of Lewis Kipperman, ma'am?"

"No. Mr. Kipperman is also an antique car buff, of which I had acquired a couple, and he bought. We became friends, as we have other antique interests in common. He has been a great help to me in that area."

"He is a good man, ma'am."

"I discern that you are, too, Rod," Claire responded.

"Call the desk if you need anything. You need only lift the phone. Your food orders will be up in about twenty minutes." He smiled as the elevator doors closed.

"Wow, Mom. It's good to have friends in high places. I feel totally safe here."

Once in their suite, Zoey called out, "Five-minute showers each and Detective Bennard will have to interview us in plush hotel robes and slippers. I will send to have our clothing cleaned."

Soon both ladies were showered and looking slick with damp hair, wearing comfy pink robes and slippers.

"That was quite an experience, Mom. There wasn't one direction that didn't have a shower head blasting with nice steamy sprays."

"Yeah, I'm glad we got to use one turn-on knob for all those. Can you imagine if we had to regulate each shower head for the right temperature?"

The doorbell chimed. "That must be the detective." Claire went to the door and pushed an intercom button. "Who is it?"

"Detectives Bennard and Smith."

She unlatched the door.

About that time, the elevator opened to the foyer with a service cart of lobster dinner for four.

"Just in time, detectives. I ordered dinner for four. Kind of a bet that you'd bring someone with you."

"We were just saying how hungry we are," said Smith with a huge smile.

The waiter impeccably set everything up at a glass table. As they ate, Smith took notes between big bites. Soon the notepad was filled, and everyone continued talking about the Koona Caves, where it was revealed the police and FBI knew something was going on, but they couldn't get the connection. The fact that there was a well tunnel was a big find.

After dinner, some lemon sherbet dessert also arrived, with almond cookies. Claire nibbled as she borrowed a laptop Smith brought. She wanted to show the detectives the cameo pin. Since Butch had pocketed it, she had to get into her email to show a picture. Fortunately, Claire had messaged the photos she took at

Mr. Belmont's from her phone to herself earlier. With great excitement, she showed the two men.

"This is amazing." Bennard scooted the screen to see from his angle. "What are these documents there, you took pictures of?"

"We don't know. I am not very good with math or chemistry. Just English," Claire admitted. "I'm an editor."

"I recognize some of it." Smith raised his eyebrows, and his face paled. "These diagrams show blueprints for nuclear fission—those are the abbreviations for plutonium and uranium, right there."

"I knew I brought *you* for a reason," Bennard said. "Hurry, slide through the other pictures. What else do you see?"

"It looks like some sort of secret code, here. Let's see. 'Go the second…'"

"Mile?" Claire offered.

"No, no." He studied it a moment longer. "Each of these phrases has a similar pattern." He grabbed his notebook and started sketching possibilities. "No, no," he muttered to himself. He sketched some more. "'Go the second nuke.' Yes, Nuke! Nuke is the word. This is more than enough evidence that there is a dirty bomb on the island!" he said to his companion.

THIRTEEN

"I didn't say anything," Bennard responded with wide eyes, "because it was only a suspicion and we couldn't prove it. But there has been Internet chatter that there is a bomb on this island somewhere."

He made a quick call to headquarters. "Get a hold of the Feds and all the people having to do with nuclear crime. IMMEDIATELY! Get ten people on this. Get Thoms, Billings and his people, and... and Roberts! Make sure Roberts calls me A.S.A.P! Okay!"

His phone soon rang. He answered and said, "Uh huh" a lot, hung up and looked at Zoey and Claire with a serious face. "Good news and bad news."

"Let's have it." Claire braced herself.

"We got the tribe you guys call *zombies* at the cavern. They are in jail. But there was no chief. I think you guys are safe staying here. I'm going to go back to the office now so I can detail work from there. Keep in touch always, even hourly, if anything out of the ordinary occurs. What is important is that you keep me posted.

You are also my eyes and ears."

"We will do that, believe me," Claire assured.

"What is your plan of procedure, detective?" Zoey asked.

"We will interview all the prisoners. And look further through those caves to see if we find more. We have to find whatever would point to a nuclear bomb, which would transcend into thousands of deaths—not just a few murders. Sorry, I didn't mean to alarm you."

"Ohhhh," Zoey took a breath and said with a rather mundane attitude, "we're used to it."

Claire blurted out a giggle in a high-pitch tone, influenced by nerves. "Sorry."

The next day, breakfast was great, and their clothes had been cleaned and returned. The bunny had investigated the entire suite and used the cat box like Zoey expected. The bunny also chewed through a lamp cord, that fortunately only had electricity if it was turned on at the wall.

Room service brought up a surprise basket of goodies for the girls. As they received the gift graciously, the doors to the elevator across from them were still open. The service man got in and pushed the button to go down. As the door had just inches left to close, the bunny shot out of the suite for a ride down.

"Mom! The bunny got out into the elevator!" called Claire.

"Let's go get him, then." Zoey headed in a trot.

As Zoey and Claire reached the bottom floor and the elevator door opened to the lobby, they spotted the little furball take yet another elevator. "That bunny!" Zoey blurted in frustration.

They ran over, but the doors closed on them. They watched numbers light up until the elevator paused and stayed on the number three. "He's on the third floor!" said Claire. They pushed the button and soon the doors opened. They pushed "three" and waited to be brought to the third level. When they got off and looked down the hallway, they were just in time to see the bunny enter a room.

The door was shut when they approached. Claire was about to go knock on the door and ask for the bunny back, but Zoey restrained her. "Wait. Not so fast. I don't think the bunny was acting randomly. Let's wait and see what happens—a stakeout so to speak."

They decided to wait around a corner, behind an ice machine, and watch until the door opened. It wasn't long until someone came out. They couldn't see his face, but he was a tall man wearing a fedora. They stepped back, allowing themselves to just peek. Since the man didn't look in their direction but went immediately to the elevators, there was no need to pretend they needed ice.

After he left, they cautiously walked down to the room. "Well, this is where the bunny is."

"Yep," answered Claire. "Would we be so fortunate to find the room open?" She tried the door. "Nope."

"But look who is coming down this way."

The maid was taking dirty towels out from rooms and leaving new towels.

"Do you have a piece of gum, Claire?"

"Yes, but why?"

"Quick, chew up all pieces you have and give it to me. We have to wait, back at the corner."

"Okay." She put four sticks into her mouth and worked to chew them up really good. "Who would have thought that this was hard work when you're in a hurry? Sort of like running through water."

Finally, the maid got to the bunny's room, unlocked the door, and went in. The door was left ajar.

"Give me the gum." Zoey held out her hand.

After she had the pink mass, she ran down the way and peeked into the room, pushing the gum into the door catch, and then ran back. Just as she rounded the corner, the maid exited, placing the dirty laundry into a plastic bag, and went on her way to the next room.

When the maid disappeared, the Kanes made a dash for it. Zoey pushed at the door. It opened. When they got inside and shut the door, they found the bunny lying on the bed. His ears perked and eyes opened, but he didn't move.

"Okay, this is our chance, sweetie. Mind your E's and threes."

"I will. You watch your P's and Q's."

They started looking around, opening drawers.

"Not too much here." Claire picked up a book that had been tucked into a nightstand drawer. "I guess they don't do Bibles anymore. This is a book on hypnotism.

129

What is the world coming to?!"

"Yeah," Zoey answered. "You can't trust who you are talking to these days because they are probably hypnotizing you."

"Puts a new spin on the reason for so many divorces these days," Claire said dryly. "People eventually *come to.*"

"That makes absolute sense," Zoey said as she slid open a closet door. "Oh-oh. Would you look at this?!" She pulled down a thirty-gallon plastic bag, feathers pluming out its opening. She reached in and retrieved the adorned gold mask, a black wig with red-beaded ornaments, and a golden cloth wrap. "Have you got chills yet?"

"Put it all back exactly as you can, Mom, so we don't alert whomever it is that owns that stuff. Then we can get the police up here."

"Are you putting two and two together yet, Claire? The bunny? The bunny at the well. The bunny in the cavern at the platform?"

"Oh my gosh!" Claire snapped a hand to her mouth in surprise. Larry the Great is a fiend!"

"Yes! That is the wildest but truest answer." Zoey nodded emphatically.

"Ladies!" a man said.

Throughout their snooping around, they hadn't been paying attention to the open door. They were totally taken by surprise.

"This is terribly unfortunate, girls. I can't let you leave here, now can I?" Larry smiled. "Oh... gum?" he said. "You two are really clever and yet so dumb."

He started to reach inside his beige silk coat for what Claire knew to be a gun. Then, another surprise!

Butch entered the room. "The door was open and..." He paused when seeing the Kanes. A look like guilt crossed his face. "Zoey and Claire? What are you two doing here?"

"They are room invasion artists." Larry finished pulling out his gun.

"Butch, you are a constant disappointment," Zoey said with a hand on her hip. "At first, I thought you just a coward. But I never figured you for a mass murderer."

"Mass murderer?" Larry said. "Oh, you must mean the nuke. Wow, I really underestimated you two. Your boyfriend is getting paid well for his loyalty."

Butch was standing next to Larry, smiling. "That I am."

Larry motioned with his weapon for the two ladies to sit down on the bed. "I'm not going to shoot you. I have a better idea."

Zoey and Claire sat down and noticed Butch had disappeared again.

Larry tied the two back to back and around a bedpost.

"I knew there was a screw loose, ever since Claire told me you didn't give her a real kiss," Zoey said.

"The first night on the cruise, Claire was a lovely part of my card trick. Later, I had to invite you two to my afterparty and get cozy, so I could see just how much you knew." He cinched the cords tighter. "My followers informed me that you two had the pin. Luckily, while I was having a meeting with my associates at The Pirate's Galley, I saw the brooch and knew the rumors were true. I went over to your table to perform a magic trick, so I could distract you while Mike snatched the pin."

"You just added another reason to my list for how guys have used me," Claire said.

"What about all the voodoo dolls following me around?" Zoey asked.

"Voodoo dolls?" He smiled. "Those are just part of the traditions I exploited to get close with the Koonas. They thought of that on their own. I just wanted them to retrieve the pin, and then out you."

"They just listened to you?" Claire said, astounded.

"Yes, they accepted me as their leader. It was quite easy." He pointed to the book on hypnotism. "I just say the words, and they follow my every command."

"What a *charmer* you turned out to be," Claire said. "What are you going to do now that you have us tied up?"

He grabbed his bag and a briefcase from the closet. "See the clock on the nightstand?"

They looked. "Yes."

"When it says 9:34, you two are dead." The clock showed 9:30.

"What? By a bomb?" Zoey asked, her brown eyes filled with fear.

"Yup." He threw his bag over his shoulder and clutched his briefcase. "It's been a pleasure, ladies. I've got a plane to catch." He exited the room.

FOURTEEN

"Where would the bomb be?" Claire asked.

"I don't know. Hurry, let's try to get out." She moved around, wiggling, and pulling, trying to release the rope's tie. Claire followed in like manner.

The clock's digital face soon switched to 9:34.

FLUSH. They heard the swishing from the restroom's toilet bowl.

With sweat on her forehead, Claire exhaled. "Well, that's not what I expected."

"We're not dead?"

"No, we're not."

Whistling, Butch exited the bathroom, wiping his hands on his pants. "Where's Larry? What did I miss?"

BOOM! They heard an explosion from somewhere not so far away.

"What was that?" Zoey demanded. "The bomb?"

"Is that what I flushed?" Butch said, raising his eyebrows.

A gush of water came flooding out from under the

bathroom door.

"Butch, I can't believe we kissed. You conniving, lying murderer."

"Where's Larry?" he asked.

"He left a minute ago. Go follow him, you lemming!"

He turned and rushed out the door.

"Bunny, would you mind nibbling at our cords?" Claire asked.

He twitched his nose and stayed lying there.

A gunshot fired, echoing throughout the hotel.

The women looked at each other, affright.

"Just kill me now," Zoey said. "I am tired of the suspense."

Another gunshot fired. They stayed quiet, listening. There was a clatter in the hall, and soon Butch returned. He was dragging something across the now soaked carpeting.

"What now?" Zoey asked, trying to see what he was pulling. "Along with me, you have come back to dump your pride?"

"Ooh, ow!" Butch winced in pain, but not from what Zoey said. He let go and pressed against his shoulder.

"Are you bleeding?" Claire could see better from her angle.

"I've been shot," he said.

"The police are here?"

"I'm here if that counts." He finished pulling in what he was dragging across the carpet.

It was Larry Potter, limp. Butch finished dragging him to the side of the bed. He pulled handcuffs out of his back pocket and linked Larry's wrists around a foot of the bed. He then put Larry's gun onto the night stand.

Zoey's voice turned sweetly embarrassed. "Butch? Who are you really?"

Butch cut through their cords with a pocketknife as he explained. "I'm with the FBI. My ID is in my wallet." He continued, "It's a good thing I've been trailing this guy and went undercover to get closer to learn more about his intentions. I'm sorry I disappointed you two, but I couldn't blow my cover. It worked out for you, 'cause I spiked his drink during the Koona ceremony and loosed you from the ropes he had you tied up with in the Koona cavern.

"I knew that those hypnotized, fake zombies wouldn't do anything that Larry here didn't tell them to do. With him asleep, they weren't going to harm anyone. Eventually, he came to enough to escape the police, who were on his trail, thanks to you two."

The ropes were released from around the two women. They rubbed their wrists, feeling a slight burn from fighting against them.

Butch, while keeping an eye on Larry the Great, made a call for a police unit. They sent three cars with lights and sirens up the driveway to the hotel. Six of them went in. As Larry was being handcuffed and taken by force, he awoke. Realizing what a predicament he was in, he called to Butch, Zoey, and Claire over his shoulder, "It's too late! It's timed to go off at twelve o'clock tonight."

"You two go back to the ship now," Butch told the Kanes. "I'll call Security ahead of time and vouch for you since you don't have your ID's. I am taking custody of the rabbit. He knows every inch of those caves like they are his second home. I'm going to follow this little guy around, hunting for where the dirty bomb is. I haven't been able to have total access, because only four other people could go into all the cave rooms: Belmont, Larry, Mike. And the other guy, Khrushchev."

Zoey and Claire took a cab back to the ship. As they boarded, security expecting them, they felt a sense of accomplishment. That was a nice warm feeling, only to be iced over by the thought that unless the nuke were discovered and disconnected, the whole island would be vaporized. They decided to go see Cher at a luncheon show.

The captain made a ship's announcement. "We will be concluding our cruise, ladies, and gentlemen, sailing from this port at 12:00 midnight. Our chefs have created an entirely new menu for you today of which you will never experience the like again. Good sailing..."

Claire was wearing a cream-colored pant and blouse combination, large gold hoop earrings, and her dark hair was sleek and shiny. Zoey wore her hair knotted at the neck with a stream of red hair down her back in a soft wave. She decided on black pants and a black pullover with a white jacket, black and white shoes, and black and white earrings, making her hair color stand out. She mascara'd her eyelashes twice.

"I am so worried about having to rely on a bunny to find the source of a nuclear bomb by twelve midnight, Mom. I can't get it out of my mind."

"I know me too. But there is nothing either of us can do. Butch has the best idea."

The Cher lookalike looked great in an extravagant Vegas-style costume. She sounded very much like her, everyone thought.

Time drifted by. Night had fallen over The Sunburst. Claire found her cell phone still in the cabin, so when it rang she was delighted to get a call. It was Butch.

"We got it!" he announced victoriously. "The bunny eventually went into every tunnel and cave. We found uranium rich ore, and even a stock of plutonium being submerged in ocean water inside the stinky cave that no one wanted to go into."

"Oh, thank goodness! That is wonderful." She turned to Zoey, who was trying to listen in. "They found it, Mom."

Butch continued, "Larry thought he was so smart, but he forgot to press the activate button. Either that or he was just trying to scare us!"

"I am *so* glad to hear that," Claire said with a wide smile. "Come back to the ship tonight. We will celebrate."

"You bet," Butch said. "I just want to know, you likey Detective Smith? He wants a date with you. Should I tell him yes?"

"Sure, he's a really nice guy."

"Done! See you around eleven."

Claire hung up and turned to her mom. "I guess we will have a little fun tonight. Butch and Smith will meet us at eleven. Yay, Mom! And yet… I'm feeling a little depressed."

"I think we have had too many near death experiences. I feel a little post-distress too. Is that it?"

"Butch said that dumb Larry didn't have the bomb activated. He was all mouth."

"Wait a minute, wait a minute, Claire. Did Larry really seem like he wasn't making a real threat? He had an awful lot of satisfaction in those words to just be fake. Think about it."

"Oh noooo, Mom! Remember the secret words 'Go the second nuke'? There must be a *second* flipping nuke. Where? What time is it?" She opened her cell phone—10:20. Then she dialed. "Stay on the job, Butch. There's another bomb." She explained her reasoning, and added, "I'm sure it's activated. Okay, keep me in the know."

FIFTEEN

"Let's go into The Sand-Drift Lounge, daughter. I feel like throwing back a root beer float."

"Yeah, let's blow the suds off a root beer! I think we should swagger in and spit on the floor, 'cause we're tough!"

"Hee hee. I double dog dare you!"

"You got it, Mom. Spit right on the floor! Never dare the kid. I just might spit in somebody's eye."

"Ten-thousand to your favorite charity if you do."

With that deal, they entered the Sand-Drift Lounge, where they discovered eight of the Red Hat Ladies in a large half-circle booth. "Hey, join us," Kathryn said.

"Yes. Let's get a couple of chairs to pull up." Matilda smiled.

Zoey and Claire found their conversation fun, yet the bomb threat was still in the forefront of their thoughts.

Eleven o'clock arrived, and one drunk man began

behaving loud and obnoxious.

"Somebody ought to eighty-six him from the bar," Kathryn said.

"Nobody is going to do that," another replied, "because that is the illustrious captain of the ship—Captain Vladimir Krucheve."

Zoey started coughing, and Claire patted her on the back. "Yeah, Mom. This looks like opportunity and a spot of good luck! Only four know about the secret room of the caves: Larry, Mike, Mr. Belmont, and *Khrushchev*. What are we going to do?"

"Okay, you two. What is going on?"

The Red Hat Ladies leaned forward for the answer.

"There is a bomb on the ship, and the captain is a conspirator," Claire blurted out matter-of-factly with a big smile.

Kathryn yelled to the waiter, "Bring a round of drinks to this table, pronto, and make them stronger with extra root in their beers." She pointed to the Kanes, then leaned forward again to hear more.

"What can anyone do?" one of them asked.

"I do have a plan." Zoey leaned forward to reveal it in a little more privacy. "A couple of you cause a commotion on the bridge, so they call back the captain. Claire and I will follow him, and hopefully, he will want to check the status of the bomb to see if it is still okay."

"Slide out, girls, and three of you come with me," Matilda commanded. "Let's do this!"

"You could all spit on the floor for strength and valor," Claire suggested and giggled.

"Nerves again, sweetie?"

"Yes, Mom."

The four Red Hat volunteers pretended to spit on the floor and strode out with long strides, set jaws and fire in their eyes. If they had any fear, it wasn't visible.

One couple had seen this and leaned out of their booth to watch them leave. The woman said, "Well, I never!"

Zoey said to Claire, "Let it go!"

Claire nodded and looked away from them, relaxing. She dialed. "Butch! The captain's name is Vladimir Krucheve. We have a plan in motion. The bomb is probably on the ship. Over and out."

Fifteen minutes later, over the entire ship's intercoms, voices could be heard arguing. A man was saying, "Give me that! No! Ow!"

"We've got another hat pin if you don't back away," a woman responded, and then became considerably louder as she spoke right into the receiver. "Captain Krucheve! We know! Your plan has run aground."

Then the intercom went dead.

The captain immediately got up from the bar with a stony look on his face. He walked fast, listing to one side in drunkenness, then corrected his way.

Zoey and Claire followed quietly. The four Red Hat Ladies who remained followed Zoey and Claire quietly. Soon, Zoey and Claire found themselves peeking around a corner to watch the captain go into his suite. The four Red Hat Ladies peeked at Zoey and Claire from around a different corner. Zoey and Claire tiptoed to the captain's door to see what he was doing. The four Red Hat Ladies tiptoed to the corner Zoey and Claire had left.

The Kanes finally entered the captain's room. He pulled out a case, opened it on his bed, and checked a timer.

There was a lamp on a nearby stand. Claire quietly unplugged it, keeping her eye on the back of the tall man. She glanced at her mom, who nodded, before hitting him across the head. He fell over and yelled out in pain.

Zoey grabbed the case and hefted it out the door. She was surprised to find the Red Hat Ladies right outside.

"Quick, hide this in your room," Zoey hurried. "It won't go off until midnight. We have some time. Run!"

Two of them ran off together, both holding on to a corner.

Back inside, Zoey found Claire wrestling the captain, who was now choking her. She spat in his eye. He went to wipe at it, breaking his hold from around her neck.

Zoey grabbed her daughter, only to be punched on the cheek and given a bloody nose by Krucheve. She fell back onto the floor.

At that moment, the two remaining Red Hat Ladies ran in and took hold of anything they could, hitting the captain from behind. The four women together started beating and kicking him down onto his bed.

"Blow everybody up, will you? Hit him again, Sally!" one said.

"Get off of me!" yelled the captain. "It's like being

pecked to death by chickens!"

The women moved back, while the older ladies held hat pins in both hands. "Don't flinch or you'll get this nasty six incher in the throat." Sally's eyes were wild.

Claire called Butch. "We are up in the captain's suite. The bomb is secured. Come at once."

Butch and Detective Smith soon came running down the hall and into the room with guns drawn. "I am amazed! You broads did a super job. Wonder women!"

"Butch is a smooth talker," explained Zoey to Sally.

Smith had the captain handcuffed, and two more men from the FBI arrived. They worked in unison to get Krucheve up and walking out the door.

"I didn't want to do it," the Russian wept. "They threatened my family."

"Extortion?" someone said.

"Where's the bomb? It would be so nice to know that," Smith said.

Sally answered, "It's in 204 with Cindy and Angelica."

He notified Bennard so the bomb could be properly taken off the ship and disarmed.

Butch turned to assess Zoey with compassion in his eyes, seeing the blood dripping down her face onto her clothes. "Have a bit of a fight, did we? Come on, Claire, let's get your mom looked at by the doc. And, geez, you all look like you were in the battle of Armageddon. Come on. Let's all go."

Sally began to cry. "Oh, I never had such fun! I don't know why I'm crying."

Butch answered, "It's your body saying, 'Never do that again!'"

"How is your shoulder?" Zoey noticed he had on a clean shirt and there was no blood.

He winked. "The bullet nicked me. It bled quite a bit, but I'm good."

It was nearing midnight, and the ship left dock early. Two exhausted vacationers, and two exhausted detectives sat on a balcony to a swank stateroom. There was a warm breeze, and the golden moonlight was peaceful as they sipped their tropical drinks.

"So, it was overexposure to plutonium that caused the spontaneous burning of the dog and crazy Mike?" Zoey said, shaking her head. "You know, a writer couldn't make this stuff up."

Everyone agreed.

"And no one would believe that a billionaire would be in debt." Claire tossed the gossip journal Zoey retrieved from Belmont's onto the small table in front of them. "But even nations can go into debt. He shouldn't have invested in such a devious plot."

The magazine landed open on a page, saying, "Is Belmont broke?"

Detective Smith, who re-introduced himself to Claire as just Gavin, put an arm around her shoulders, pulling her closer. Butch was about to do the same with Zoey, but the sound of the cabin door opening caused the four to jump in nervousness.

It was the Red Hat Society with a housekeeping key. They brought drinks, sundaes, chips and dip, and laughter.

Kathryn smiled. "Tomorrow you snuggle. Tonight, we have some fun together, for we may never see each other again."

The four got up and joined their friends in the sitting room.

"Oh no, what time is it?" Butch suddenly glanced at his watch.

"The bomb is gone, it's okay!" Zoey said. "Must be aftershock."

"No, I'm going to be late for my dance routine!"

"You mean, you really do have to perform tonight?" Claire asked.

"Yes, of course."

The Starlight Room's pink stage lights turned on, highlighting a tall sailing ship. The crowd was exuberant, clapping in anticipation. Claire sat with Gavin in the front row, smiling. He was next to a long row of Red Hat Ladies. There was no sight of Zoey anywhere.

Butch was high up to the right of the stage, on an elevated stand, hidden by what remained of the open curtain. He was wearing a pirate's hat, gold hoop earrings, and a white blouse, exposing his muscular chest. Stepping up with a black boot, he grabbed a rope with one arm, and with his other, he threw a redhead over his broad shoulders.

"You ready for this, woman with hair like soft fire?" he asked.

SIXTEEN

Tropical drinks, white sand, and island men now behind them, the Kanes felt a little home sick. Especially after they made a three-day pitstop to peruse Indiana's First Annual Indoor Garage Sale. The fairgrounds hosted more than fifty-thousand square feet of odds and ends from homes, farms, and even businesses. Now sitting in their taxi, taking them to Hillgate Manor, they mostly kept to themselves, thinking over all of the recent, crazy happenings.

The sky was darker than when they had left. Soft breezes stirred leaves around trees, benches, and lamp posts. They passed the famous Homestyle Buffet, with its perpetually packed parking lot, knowing they were getting closer.

Claire laughed to herself once again, thinking of what her mother had purchased at the garage sale.

"You're not still thinking of the llama, are you?" Zoey said with a small smile, sitting to Claire's left.

"I still can't believe you got it. A llama fountain that spits water?"

"That will be so fun for our side yard, don't you think?" Zoey's light-brown eyes sparkled in delight. "It will be delivered tomorrow."

"You're funny, Mom."

"I know, the motion detector that you purchased was way more practical." Zoey patted her daughter's knee lovingly.

"Hey, I bought something weird too."

"Oh, what was that?" Zoey's eyebrows went up.

"The stuffed cat with an eye patch who hisses."

Zoey nodded. "The dogs are going to love that."

The taxi soon entered through the hauntingly heavy old gate that surrounded their eighty acres and headed uphill on a paved drive. The Fillmore cemetery, and accompanying memorial museum, was a pretty sight amidst fall leaves.

"I gave Matilda our address," Zoey said. "It just so happens, she lives not too far from here."

"Really?" Claire said. "You think you'll visit her."

"Sure, maybe someday."

Even with a few dark and looming clouds in the sky, Hillgate Manor gleamed bright white, as if happy to see them home. The taxi parked at the front door, which opened right away. Their Estate Manager, Max, stepped out and waved, wearing a T-shirt and blue jeans over his wiry old body. He was followed by two Dobermans, Gunner in his spike collar, and Bond in his bowtie. The dogs wagged their bobtails as they approached the car.

The cabby hesitated at opening his door, evidently fearful.

"They're good dogs," Claire assured him. "Well-trained."

The Kanes exited, saying hello to Max and leaning down to hug their handsomely sleek pets. "We missed you," Zoey cooed, kissing Bond's forehead.

The cabby set the suitcases out, and Max quickly took them from there. Claire paid for their ride, adding a twenty-dollar tip, and the Kanes entered their manor with wide smiles, smelling the distinct scent of owning a beautiful mansion filled with antique décor.

Zoey spread her arms out and twirled, looking up at the large chandelier hanging from the high ceiling. Claire copied her, laughing at their childish behavior. Gunner and Bond trotted around them, lightly barking in happiness.

"It's a dream living here, isn't it?" Zoey said.

"Yes," Claire answered, still spinning.

Suddenly serious, Zoey put her hands on her hips. "Meet me in the sunroom, darling. We'll have breakfast toast and talk about some things."

"Talk? Is everything okay?" Claire asked, trying to discern the look on her mother's face.

"Yes." Zoey nodded. "I'll grab the toast while you grab the mail that Max collected while we were away." She turned and walked toward the kitchen. "See you soon."

"Okay." Claire retrieved the stack of mostly junk mail from the foyer's marble table.

Back in the sunroom, Autumn sunlight bathed the space consisting of a long, antique table with a lace runner. Zoey served their saucers of nine-grain wheat toast with marmalade. Claire set the mail between them and thanked her mother for the snack.

Zoey sat, concern creasing her brow. "Are you still going to pursue journalism?"

Claire paused mid-bite, raising her eyebrows. She finished chewing and said, "I don't know, Mother. What are you thinking?"

"I had so much fun solving mysteries with you at Kinikiwiki."

"Yeah, so did I." Claire's eyes narrowed a touch. "But what does that have to do with journalism?"

"I was just thinking," Zoey said, tossing a hand up. "I know you wanted to work for Felix Belmont before all manner of mayhem went down. But instead, maybe we can continue solving mysteries. Not just for fun, but as a vocation."

"Oh, I don't know about that," Claire said. "Haven't you had enough heart-stopping adventures for a while? I don't even know if anyone can truly call us private eyes... or sleuths... detectives. Whatever they call people who want to do what you're proposing. We've just *bumbled* into trouble."

"That's true," her mother said with a sigh. Now it was apparent that disappointment was shining in her eyes, as they turned red and a touch watery.

"Oh, what's wrong?" Claire set a hand on her mother's wrist. "What did I say?"

Zoey wiped a tear that spilled from her eye. "It's just good to have you around again. I missed you when you lived in New York. Finding Hillgate, and turning it into a hotel together, made me really happy. Now that we aren't doing that, I was thinking of the next best thing, is all."

Claire turned in her chair and wrapped her arms around her mother, hugging her for a long moment. When she pulled back, she said, "You're my best friend, Mom. Right now, more than ever, we need each other. So, if it helps, I'll start with Riverside's local media. Maybe I can get a job with Bob and The Daily Bugle, or Lucas, with Channel 2 News. No more New York for me."

They sat back, seemingly satisfied. Claire rifled through the mail, tossing what would be thrown away to the side. She paused in pleasant surprise over one letter in particular. "Oh, look—a letter from Matilda Dread." Claire took a butter knife to open the envelope, as her mother chewed her breakfast toast, leaning forward with interest.

Quickly scanning the letter, Claire knew her mother was going to get her wish. Another mystery, this time involving a map discovered in a mansion, and a decrepit finger bone tied to it. Claire smiled uncontrollably. Perhaps the Kanes were meant to be sleuths, after all. The game was afoot.

The end.

SUN SPIRIT TEMPLE

(A CRUISE TO MURDER SHORT STORY)

Arrival at Kinikiwiki island was filled with the anticipation of fun in the sun, tropical fruit drinks, excellent island excursions, and lots of adventure. Zoey and Claire entered their luxury cabin aboard The Sunburst, ready to change clothes for ship activities. Maybe a nap first.

They had spent all morning out. The two thought about ordering something in to drink instead of lunch because they were still too full from their pulled-pork brunch. It had come with pineapple-coconut rice (sweet and yummy), and poi (on the bland side), poi being the island's staple, much like potatoes.

Zoey removed her blouse. She was about to remove her jeans, too, but paused when her fingers raked over the folded paper she had stuffed in her back pocket—Penny's Underground Excursions list. Even though the Kanes had made a truce with Penny, months ago, there was still something a little suspicious about the woman.

Her smile often curled a touch, hinting at her remaining desire to pull one over on them.

It could be a challenge keeping up with Penny's antics. The latest was obvious, however. The auburn-haired friend had warned the Kanes of zombies. Zoey shook her head again at the thought.

Claire fell onto the bed to rest, her brunette hair fanning around her pretty face. "This place is too fun," she said with a dreamy sigh.

Still in her bra and jeans, Zoey approached an armoire in search of a shirt. A loud, threatening pounding sounded at the cabin door. She instinctively bolted for her purse. She needed her gun.

Claire shot up in fear. "I spoke too soon."

The pounding increased in strength. A fist broke through. Zoey aimed and pulled the trigger to her little .22 semi-automatic, but nothing shot out. She tried again, with no success. Looking down at her gun in bewilderment, she wondered if she had somehow bought a fake, a toy, by mistake.

The pale man burst completely through, bringing with him a reeking, rotting stench. "Aaargghhh!"

Claire snatched the lightweight summer blanket off her mother's bed and threw it over the zombie's head. He beat at it with his sickly moan, giving the Kanes little time to sprint by him in their high heels to across the hall.

They desperately knocked on The Red Hat Society's cabin. No one answered, but the door swung open. The two hurried in and locked it in terror, thinking the anemic man with dark circles around his eyes would only break this door down as well.

From the hall, another man's voice became audible. "Hey! What's going on up here?" he said in irritation. "Hey, you! Did you break this door down?"

"Aarrgghh."

"Don't give me attitude, buddy! I don't care what your girlfriend did."

"Aaargghh. Aaargghh."

"Get out! You deserve what you got. Your teeth look disgusting. Take a tip; no woman is going to go for a guy with bad hygiene!"

"Eergghh."

"Crying won't help."

"Aaargghhh!!!"

"Go on, get out now! You'll have to pay for that door!"

Zoey and Claire placed ears against the door to listen further. It all seemed quiet now. They turned around and stared in concern. Various styles of red hats laid all over the floor, chaotically arrayed.

"What happened in here?" asked Claire with suspicion. "This is way weird." She cautiously stepped around the hats, trying to make sense of things.

Zoey picked up a slip of paper off a bed. "Well, what have we here?" Jagged red-marker writing read, "PiNk Hats! DoN't cOme uP to tHe SuN SpiRit TemPle!!! At ALL! Aaargghh!!!"

"Is this for real?" Claire asked. Mom and daughter stood looking at each other with worry. A knock at the door made them jump.

"Who is it?" Zoey didn't move a muscle.

"Doreen, your daughter."

Claire went ahead and opened the door. "Your mom isn't here. No one is."

"Nice red bra," the blonde Pink Hatter said upon entering and seeing Zoey. Fuchsia lace draped off her 20's-inspired hat, and over one eye. "Macy's?" she asked.

Claire promptly shut and locked the door, while quipping, "Yeah, my mom is a bad influence on me."

"Oh," said Zoey, looking down at herself. "Well, it is what it is. We ran over here to escape an intruder." Her eyes cast about for something to cover herself up with.

Doreen surveyed the scene before her, stepping around the red hats. "An intruder? At your cabin? Did he do this too?" she asked.

"We don't exactly know," Claire said, rubbing her wrist. Dare she mention zombies of all things?

"Well, the Pink Hats had invited The Red Hats to open seating in the Sand Drift Lounge for lunch. When they didn't show, I thought I'd come check in on things. Nobody's answering their cell phones."

Zoey gave up on covering herself. "Were you all, by chance, planning an after-lunch outing to the Sun Spirit Temple?" she asked, trying to make a connection to the bizarre note she'd found.

"Sun Spirit Temple?" the Pink Hatter repeated. "Yes, but not today."

"Maybe something happened. The intruder at our

cabin was a... um... zombie. Perhaps a zombie—" Zoey paused with a sigh. She could hear how absurd her own words were sounding.

"Oh, the rumors of zombies," Doreen said with lighthearted amusement. "You must be describing an act. You know, for entertainment."

"Oh, yeah?" Zoey said with dry irritation. "Well, how many jokes have you seen break down a door?" She opened the cabin and swung an arm toward their suite across the hall.

Doreen looked but laughed. "You guys play a pretty good game. Cut it out now, you teasers." She laughed some more. "But, hey, why don't you two join us at our table tonight? I've seen you two befriending The Red Hatters, so I'm sure they'd love the idea."

Instead of responding, the duo turned to see why the Pink Hatter would laugh at such a destructive scene as their busted-up door. To their surprise, it was intact, nothing wrong.

Doreen went on her way down the hall. "My mom said you two were a lot of fun. I'll go look for her at the pool. She's probably swimming and forgot about the time."

Zoey approached their door for a better look. Claire scanned up and down the hallway, not so sure the zombie wasn't on his way back to get them, dragging one leg behind him in a ghoulish walk.

"That's a new door," Zoey said, touching it.

"I'm going to report what happened." Claire took her phone out of her pocket and dialed. "My phone isn't working. No call is going through." She put it away. "There's a map on Penny's excursion pamphlet, isn't there, Mom?"

"Yes. I think we have to take a little trip to Sun Spirit Temple."

Their card no longer worked with their new door. "That is just lovely!" Clare said, perplexed. "None of this makes any sense."

A woman at the customer service desk was happy to help. She searched the system and found that The Red Hatters had all checked out to the island the night before and hadn't yet returned. "People often spend the night on the island," she said. "I'm sure everything's fine."

The Kanes knew different. "Where's a cowboy when we need him?" Zoey asked Claire, stepping away for a private moment. "I really don't want to go chasing the dead. That's nuts!"

"Mother, you really need to put a shirt on," Claire said. "Walking around the ship in your *bra* is nuts!"

Zoey looked down at her chest and quickly covered up with her hands. "What's wrong with me? Did anyone notice? Do you think people thought it was a bikini top?"

Rather than answer, Claire said, "Hurry over here."

They entered one of the ship's stores, hosting all sorts of T-shirts and souvenirs. Claire pulled a T-Shirt off its hanger and shoved it toward her mother. "Try this."

"I survived The Great Volcano Dip," it read in zombie-like penmanship.

"I thought that was one of the *secret*, underground excursions," Zoey said.

"Just put it on and buy it, Mom, secret or no," Claire said in impatience.

Zoey slipped it over her head. It was rather large, but she was in a hurry to be modest, so it didn't really matter. They quickly purchased it, excited to go search for their missing friends.

On the way out of the ship, Claire turned to her mother again with a disapproving glare. "Mother!"

"What? What?" Zoey asked, her heart leaping. She looked down to see she still wore the volcano shirt. But now she had no pants? "What the heck?! How did that happen!"

"At least your shirt's big, otherwise everyone would see your butt!"

"If it can pass for beachwear, I'm not doing a thing about it!"

"It will pass," Claire said, taking a drag from a cigar.

Zoey paused her steps and placed a hand of concern on her daughter's arm. "Since when did you start smoking, Claire?"

Claire eyed the big brown cancer stick with a critical eye but ultimately shrugged. "I guess since you started going pantless."

"Touché."

Claire took another drag. Her lashes fluttered over savoring it. "Weird. But I like it. It tastes like chocolate."

They continued down the ramp, neither one aware that the new T-shirt was tucked into Zoey's underwear.

"I'm starting to wonder if Larry Potter hypnotized us," she said.

At the island, Zoey stopped a tourist with black and rock-solid wavy hair. This man was a person of interest, down to his thin mustache and sleek tuxedo. "Excuse me, do you know how we'd get to Sun Spirit Temple?" she asked.

He turned and gestured toward a bus stop in the distance. "That bus will take you up most of the way. A guide will lead you from there. You better hurry." A strange smiled emerged. "You don't want to miss out on all the *fun*."

"Thank you," Claire said, her eyes narrowed at him in suspicion.

As they jogged, Zoey commented with levity, "I think we just met the devil, dear."

The bus sat parked where the faded boardwalk met a gravel road. The yellow peeking between brown rust hinted at a time it once carried happy children to school. Now it took nervously excited adults to mysterious excursions.

The Kanes climbed the stairs and paused. The bus hosted only a few other travelers. Claire found a seat without stuffing or springs pushing through tears. Their journey took them along bumpy, potholed roads, occasionally tossing the passengers up like a cob salad. No comment came from the driver. He stayed hunched over the steering wheel as he drove on.

After twenty minutes, a light sweat dotted Claire's forehead. She fanned herself with a hand. "It's so hot in here," she told her mother.

Zoey stood and worked with all her might to lower their window, but it was no use. She finally slumped down and hit it with a fist.

After nearly an hour, the bus ride was thankfully over, and the driver yelled back. "Sun Spirit Temple! Everyone else, onward to Tingler Falls!"

Zoey and Claire stepped down and off the rickety bus, relieved to feel a cool breeze whisper across their faces, and tickle up the hair at the back of their necks. The bus took off, leaving a black cloud of exhaust. When the smog dissipated, a clown stood before them, holding a walking stick and smiling.

Claire jumped back with a yelp, startled. Zoey recoiled as well, but not out of fear. He definitely needed some makeup lessons. His blood-red lipstick was smeared way outside of the black-painted lines of an exaggerated smile.

"Sorry," he said, "I have another job as a clown for kids' birthdays. My name is Terry. I'm your guide." He wore hiking boots, blue socks, cut-off jeans, and a white T-shirt. When the ladies didn't answer, he coaxed, "Off we go then?"

Zoey grinned, because what else was she going to do?! "Yes," Zoey said. "Off we go."

The clown turned to go. Claire took hold of her mother's wrist like she was still recovering from the surprise. "I hate clowns," she said into her mother's ear.

"Even the one I got you on your sixth birthday?"

"Especially that one."

"Oh, come on. Boinky was cute." Zoey chuckled.

"His big red shoe fell off during the show, and his bare foot was the same exact shape and size!"

"No need to discriminate based on feet." Zoey shrugged a shoulder. "I have a birthmark on my left foot, and your middle toes are longer than your big toes."

"Never mind, Mother, you're missing my point. Clowns are creepy. All of them."

They stepped through soggy earth of tall grasses until they came to a small lake. Their guide stretched a hand forward and invited them into a rowboat. The mother and daughter sat side by side on the back wood-plank seat. The clown took the middle and began rowing, facing them. Claire supposed his goofy smile and overlapping teeth were supposed to be endearing, but diverted her sights to the forest green water and lush vegetation surrounding it.

"You're our guide." Zoey decided to make a little friendly conversation. "So, I guess you know quite a bit about this temple we're going to. Is it overrun with zombies and The Red Hat Society?"

His smile left. "The Red Hat Society... sounds dangerous."

"Have you ever seen any zombies up at the temple?" she asked, hoping he'd say no.

"I've only heard about them, of course," he said. "See the building through the trees, there? The temple is right on that shore."

The square top-story of what looked like a beige sandstone structure rose above a mass of tall, broad-leaf foliage, held up by a couple time-worn, eroding pillars.

"What kills zombies?" Zoey asked him. "Do you know?"

"I'm a clown who specializes in balloon animals. What do I know of evil?" One eye twitched, like a tell in poker. What was he hiding?

The clown let go of the oars and suddenly dove out of the boat and into the water.

"What's he doing?" Claire asked, looking over the edge.

Zoey asked, "Was it something I said?"

The Kanes peered around, hoping to find him coming up for air, but after two minutes, then three, Claire said, "I have never heard of anyone holding their breath for longer than four minutes." She didn't know what was scarier—the clown's company, or suddenly being alone with her mother by the zombie temple.

A couple dragonflies buzzed by. Other than that, there was silence.

Claire turned back to her mother. "I'm not going to jump in and swim around the bottom of a lake, looking for a clown who wanted to commit suicide. I'll take us to shore."

When they reached their destination, Claire placed the oars inside the boat, and Zoey helped pull it on the shore.

Claire rubbed her hands in trepidation. "Mom, at

this point, anyone would say we're completely crazy for continuing on to that temple."

"I admit, I've got the heebie jeebies. After all we've already been through on this island, I don't want to go, and I don't want you to go either."

"Okay, that's how I'm feeling." Claire shielded the sun from her eyes, her brow furrowing. "Maybe we can call and tell Detective Smith our worries."

"Don't you mean *Gavin*?" Zoey teased with a big smile.

"Mother, don't *Gavin* me," Claire said, mimicking the swooning tone. "We had a little fun, but I'm actually looking forward to meeting back up with Lucas, at home, for our date."

"That's good." Her mother nodded in approval. "I like that vampire enthusiast."

Claire pulled her phone out of her pocket and dialed Smith. But when she'd press the number three, it'd show on her screen as two or five. She tried again, and it came up, this time, as six. "I don't know what's wrong. Look." She showed her mom what was happening.

Zoey took the cell and typed nine-one-one, but it came out as one-two-three. "It's broken, and I don't have my phone on me."

"Why is that, Mother?" Claire said in irritation, rubbing some of her hair away from her face. "You always forget to keep your phone handy. Now, mine is acting possessed, and we have no other option."

"Let's just push the boat in, and we'll go back to the ship." Zoey leaned over in her T-shirt and took hold of the wooden edge.

Rather than help, Claire said in a scared tone, "Uh, Motherrrrr."

Out from the trees came several women, pale, dried-up and bruised. A variety of runway-ready red hats adorned their messy hair, some with veils, some with feathers, some with glitter. They walked stiff-legged, a few jutting their arms straight out for balance.

"Just think, dear," Zoey said, clutching her daughter's shoulder, "that could have been us in that crowd."

The Kanes pulled very hard on their boat to get it in the water again. It wasn't working so well, being in such a hurry. Fast wasn't fast enough.

The zombies moaned. "Aaargghh"

Zoey yelled, "Hey!"

They all stopped and said in unison, "Uhn?"

Zoey's eyes squinted. She yelled through clenched teeth, "I don't believe in you!"

"Uhn?"

"And, ladies," she added with a hand on her hip in attitude, "there are very ugly, dried-up women wearing your red hats!"

They turned and looked each other over with their sunken-in, wide eyes. Upon them seeing all the other, hideous, women wearing their beautiful hats, they clawed at each other's hair in disapproval.

Claire's phone rang. The zombies looked around, too stupid to know what the tone meant and then continued grabbing at hats. Seeing it was her ex, Jack, calling again, Claire finally answered in a huff. "You won't stop calling me, and you don't leave any messages. What do you want?"

"Nice to hear you too," Jack said, offended. "Listen, Claire. We need another chance. You know you need me. You can't survive without my brawn and brains."

Her annoyance over such gall was suddenly greater than any fear of the living dead.

"Sorry Jack, I don't take prisoners. No mercy, no chances!"

One of the zombie women broke away from the rest, obviously interested in the Kanes. Her red hat sat precariously atop stringy hair, heavily-lined bloodshot eyes featured beneath the brim.

"Wait a moment," Claire said with a mischievous sparkle in her dark eyes. "I *do* have a glamour queen for you to meet. And she just *loves* brains! Just a moment." Claire jogged toward the zombie.

The zombie stopped dragging a foot in their direction. "Uhn?" she asked.

"Oh, don't worry." Claire stepped through some ferns to reach her. "I have a handsome man on the phone who would like a date with you." She handed the smelly woman the phone.

The phone was received with a hand of cardboard-y fingers adorned with long burgundy fingernails. Her voice was dry, crackling out, "Ulo? I whhould luuv diinnnner. Aarrgghhh."

Claire took the phone back and reassured the woman. "I'll set it up, sister. You will love him." She ran back to the boat, and the now-satisfied zombie rejoined the others.

"So," said Jack to Claire, "you want to set me up with a hot-to-trot, deep-voiced, man-huntin' lover. Maybe I'll just take you up on that." He hung up.

Claire returned to the objective at hand: scramming. The Kanes tugged hard at their boat again and finally got it to slide into the water. They clamored in, and Claire began to paddle away, her slender arms quickening like propellers.

"You do this rather well, dear," Zoey said, not thinking to question how her daughter suddenly became Speedy Gonzalez.

"I did some rowing in college," Claire said, not even breaking a sweat. "I wasn't as good as some of the girls, but it comes in handy now."

Terry the clown's maniacal face bobbed out of the water in their path, ahead of them. He tilted his head back, spouting water from his mouth like a blowhole, and then looked at Claire with a disturbing giggle. Zoey stole one of the oars from Claire, and when they came right up next to him, she conked him on the crown of his head. Down he went. This happened a couple more times, until nothing more appeared but his last breath's bubbles.

"That was the best game of Whack-A-Mole I've ever seen," Claire complimented, snatching the oar back. "Thank you for saving me."

Zoey tilted her head. "I now see what you mean, about clown's being creepy."

"Yes, Mother." Claire's arms became nothing but blurs in motion.

"Can you row even faster, sweetie? ...Row faster ...Row faster."

The boat started rocking. "Wake up, Mom! Wake up!" It was Claire, pushing on Zoey's shoulder.

Zoey sat up, rubbing her eyes. She was in her bed aboard The Sunburst. "Oh, I'm so glad you took rowing in college."

"I took Journalism." Claire sat beside her. "There was no rowing at my college. You were dreaming."

"Well, that explains a lot." She blinked.

"Like what?" Claire eyed her.

Zoey rattled off, "Why my gun didn't work, your phone wouldn't dial, I was topless, then pantless, you took up smoking stogies, the clown wouldn't drown, and you had propeller arms. Not to mention, The Red Hat Zombies, of whom you set one up on a date with Jack... for dinner." She took a breath.

Claire patted her Zoey's head. "Everything's back to normal, Mother."

Zoey raised a finger of determination. "By the way, have you told Jack off yet?"

"I did last night after you fell asleep." Claire smiled.

Shifting taller in bed, Zoey said, "So I missed out on how it all went down."

"You know me," Claire said. "I very maturely and eloquently told him to bug off. Then I slapped him with the threat of getting a restraining order."

The Kanes spent the rest of the afternoon aboard ship. The Red Hatters were in the hallways, in the restaurants, taking pictures, and playing games on deck, like ping pong and shuffleboard. None of them had a daughter named Doreen.

Zoey thanked her daughter for coming with her on that nightmare, so she didn't have to deal with that on her own. "It was awful!"

Claire said, "No problem. Anytime you need me."

The two of them went into the ship's souvenir shop to see if Zoey could buy an "I survived The Great Volcano Dip" T-shirt, but of course, there wasn't any. Instead, she was offered the "I survived The Koona Caves" T-shirt. She bought it.

Passing by the bakery, a poster stole their attention. It was of a bride and groom atop a three-tiered wedding cake. The hard-haired man who'd directed the duo to the bus turned out to be the plastic groom. Doreen stood beside him, smiling.

"But what about the clown, Mom?" Claire asked.

"I don't know." Zoey shook her head.

A man passing by whistled. "Hey, babies. Weddings are passé. Parties are in. Come to my cabin tonight. I'll tell ya how to get there."

"Hhheck no," warned Zoey, cocking her hip. "You better sober up before you fall overboard."

"You are no fun at all." He waved bye to the two pretty ladies.

"Is that your wife?" Claire called after him.

He spun around. "Where?!" Quickly realizing he'd been outed, he complained, "You two are mean girls."

The Kanes continued comfortably on their way toward the dining room, giggling every once in a while. "Yeah, he's the clown all right," Claire said dryly.

The end.

More books by the authors:

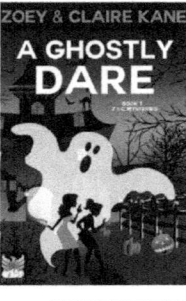  

PUBLICATIONS

Mysteries

Z & C Mysteries:
The Riddles of Hillgate
Cruise to Murder
Hexes and X's
Legend of The Lost
A Grave Situation
The Howliday Inn
A Ghostly Dare
What the Dead Said

The Dead Ex Files:
Unwed & Dead
A Model Murder
Blackjack Magic Murder

A Charli Chan Mystery:
A Yen for Murder
Lights, Camera, Murder

The Menopause Murder Society:
The Demise of The Lotto Queen
The Revenge of Pooky Poo

Contemporary Paranormal Westerns

<u>Outlaws and Fast Draws:</u>
San Francisco Stickup
Sacramento Standoff
Washington Showdown

Paranormal Romances

Head Over Halo
To Catch a Fox

Phoenix Prime Anthologies

Against the Tide
Anthousa, Xanthousa, Chrisamalousa
Babes in the City
Fairy Ointment
Haunted Hearts
Journal with a View: July – August – September
Phoenix Fantasy
Prime Fiction

PHOENIX PRIME

Author Claire Kane and this mystery series became a part of Phoenix Prime.

Phoenix Prime is a Ph.D. level workshop that spans approximately four months. It uses applied industrial psychology to address components of writing, marketing, branding, business and contract issues, productivity, etc. that combine Creative Writing and business perspectives.

The participants create a portfolio to showcase their work alongside students in doctoral programs in several major universities. The objective, in addition to expanding the professional growth of all the participants, is to study the impact of the independent author-publisher on the commercial fiction industry.

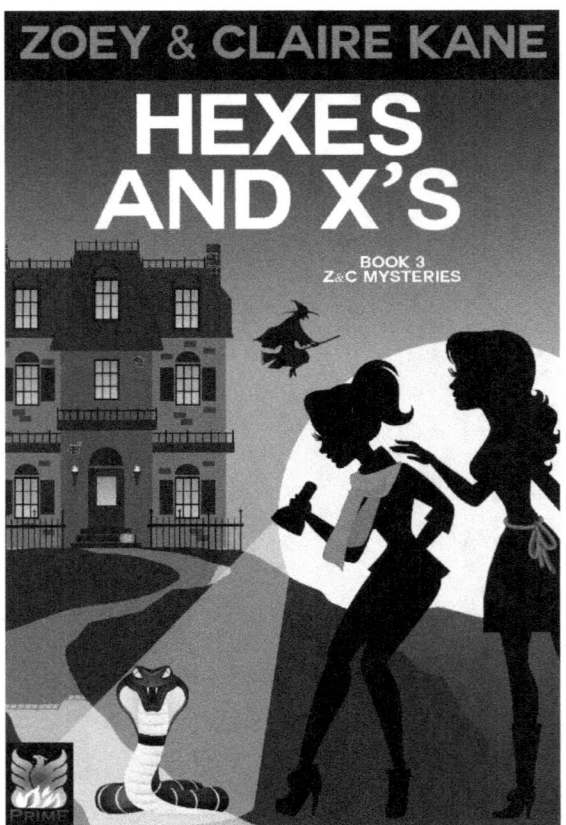

ZOEY & CLAIRE KANE

HEXES AND X'S

BOOK 3
Z&C MYSTERIES

Hexes and Xs

Z & C Mysteries, Book 3

John squinted at Debbie, as if seeing her for the first time. He exercised his jaw back and forth in annoyance. "The treasure is mine."

"Okay, hon. Just come with me and lie back down."

With one last hurrah, he turned back to everyone, raised his arms crookedly in the air, and proclaimed, "The treasure is… MINE!"

Lightning flashed, spotlighting the scene. John fell to the floor with a THUD, accentuated by thunder's BOOM!

The kitchen returned to its gloomy, dimly-lit atmosphere. All were silent, until a timid Anne Lane of the town council said, "Maybe he was murdered. Maybe you murdered him, Ms. Debbie." Eyeing the guests in the room warily, she added, "I don't trust any of you." And it was no wonder. Some actually looked elated to see John was dead.

One who wore a pleased grin was Pat. "Oh, so sorry fer the loss o' yer fiancé, Cynthia dear."

"Shove it!" The witch picked up her pen and paper.

"Every man for himself!" announced Judge Huff. "Lawbreakers will be hanged. Get on with the map, Ms. Kane."

CONTACT LINKS

Sign up for our newsletter:
http://zoeyandclaire.blogspot.com/p/loading.html

Website: zoeyandclaire.blogspot.com

Publisher's website: breezyreads.com

Facebook: fb.me/zoeyandclaire

Twitter: @Zoey_Claire

EMAIL: breezyreads@gmail.com

Merchandise and more: phoenixprimerising.com

ABOUT THE AUTHORS

Claire Kane is an avid reader and writer, who enjoys going on adventures with her eccentric mother. She's a connoisseur of classic fashion statements, craves a good root beer float, and always eats with her mouth closed. of course, she also has a weak spot for murder mysteries.

Zoey Kane has dabbled in modeling, is a licensed real-estate agent, seeks for treasures (great and small), and is often underestimated. Her free spirit complements her daughter's more analytical personality.

Together, Zoey and Claire are a mother-daughter mystery solving duo. During their downtime, they dream of island men whisking them away.

(Zoey and Claire are also fictional, but their authors are a real-life mother and daughter who use their names as pseudonyms. Don't tell them that, though.)